WINTER'S STALKER

WINTER BLACK SERIES: SEASON TWO BOOK SEVEN

MARY STONE

MARY STONE PUBLISHING

Copyright © 2024 by Mary Stone Publishing

All rights reserved.

No part of this book may be reproduced in any form or by any electronic or mechanical means, including information storage and retrieval systems, without written permission from the author, except for the use of brief quotations in a book review.

Created with Vellum

To those who stand by me in every dark twist and turn. Your support is the light that keeps me writing.

DESCRIPTION

You know what you did. So do I.

The man who's been stalking Private Investigator Winter Black is dead, but he wasn't working alone. Threats linger in the shadows, and she can't shake the chilling feeling that she's being watched.

It's about to get personal…again.

A flyer advertising her business—Black Investigations—was found on the tenth-floor balcony of a woman who apparently jumped to her death. Except Winter has never seen the brochure before. Stranger still, her two newest clients received the same fake flyer, along with a blackmail letter.

Pay for your crime or kill yourself.

Did the dead woman receive the same threat and choose option two? Or did someone make that choice for her?

As Winter digs deeper into her clients' dark confessions and pasts, she finds more questions than answers—and a terrifying pattern. Someone is playing a twisted game, and the flyers are an invitation for Winter to play…whether she wants to or not. But it's hard to win when you don't know the rules. Or your opponent.

The stakes have never been higher in Winter's Stalker, the darkly addictive seventh book in the Winter Black Season Two series, where one thing becomes chillingly clear: in this game, there are fates worse than death.

1

Clarissa Toler took a sip of her red wine and wrinkled her nose. At forty-two, she'd earned the right to drink fresh wine. She should dump this swill and uncork a new bottle, but she couldn't bring herself to bother.

She was comfortable on her back porch, despite the blurry night sky. When she was young, her parents used to take her out to the lake house in summers. Some of her favorite memories happened under the stars on the gently swaying dock. Her father, an enthusiastic amateur astronomer, would point out constellations and planets and tell her stories of ancient gods.

Here in the city, all those secrets were hidden behind smoke and ambient light. After an hour on her balcony, she still hadn't counted more than a dozen stars. The only constellation was the faded outline of the Big Dipper. Even Polaris was hiding.

Divorced from the land and divorced from the heavens. The modern world was as disconnected as it was connected. Stars used to guide the way—they were the universal navigational system. Somehow, humans had managed to render them obsolete too.

A tear slid down her cheek, which she didn't bother to wipe away. Its warmth was something real, like a twinkling star forcing its way through a gray sky.

The lake house was on her mind—memories throbbing like a pulled muscle. She couldn't remember her little brother stargazing with the family, but Clark must've been there. At least for a little while. Or maybe he was too young then, tucked away in bed while the rest of them got to stay up.

That was so long ago. She was an accomplished, modern woman now. One of the lucky few who not only enjoyed her work as an author and illustrator of children's books but was well paid for it too.

None of her young fans knew the truth behind her fanciful prose and fairy pictures. And her editor and publisher didn't understand that she was good at what she did because she was still just a twelve-year-old girl trapped in a moment she could never escape. Every time she sat down at a blank page, she was trying to find her way back to the last time she felt fully alive. If she could recreate it, maybe she could relive it.

Maybe she could get it right.

Another tear, another sip of crappy wine. Clarissa's knees felt weak, but she gripped the railing to hold herself up.

Almost thirty years had passed since the day that changed everything—the day her brother died. She'd never told a soul what happened. If she revealed the truth to her parents, they'd never forgive her. Not that she deserved forgiveness, but they didn't deserve that pain. She held it in like the final gasping breath before a plunge into dark water.

Air caught in her throat like thorns. She closed her eyes

and set down her wine, lifting the threatening note in her other hand so she could read it again.

She didn't understand how it was possible that someone had discovered her secret. No one had been there that day. The memory of her brother's dark hair bobbing in the waves, his hands reaching up. The sound of her own screams as she fought to save him.

The water was freezing, and her legs seized up. She'd been frantic, trying to get to Clark, but before she could reach him, he was gone.

After that, she lied to her parents, lied to herself. But now a stranger had found out the truth. In a way, she was relieved. Holding it in for so long had warped the memory into something strange and distant, almost like a dream. When she replayed the day Clark died, it was as if she were severed from the event, watching it play out in a locked attic room through a rusty keyhole.

Words had power. The power to create change.

As an author, Clarissa knew that to be true. But silence had power too. The power to erase. And forgetting was the only way she'd survived this long.

Ever since she checked the mail and found the note—along with a few bills and a flyer for some private detective agency, Black Investigations—Clarissa had been trying to identify who sent it. Now she realized it didn't really matter.

With one last glance at the stars, Clarissa set down her wine and stood. She leaned out over her balcony and peered down at the ten-story drop. More than enough to guarantee she wouldn't end up in the hospital recovering from injuries. That was really what she was afraid of. It wasn't the dying, but the possibility of surviving.

Clarissa had already lived through enough pain. She was sick of finding new and creative ways of hiding from it. Therapy, writing, alcohol, sex, shopping. All the things she purported to "enjoy." There was no joy in any of it, just a momentary distraction from the memory of what she'd done. What she *hadn't* done the day her baby brother drowned before her eyes while she did nothing to save him.

It was time to end it. Her parents would be sad. Her agent, maybe.

"Nobody will miss you, if that's why you're hesitating."

She clamped her hands over her ears, as if she could keep the voice inside her head from being birthed into reality. It came from deep within her mind, scraping against the walls of her consciousness with a jagged, gravelly edge. Its home was somewhere dark and festering, oozing through her thoughts, leaving scorched trails behind each word.

The voice was low and guttural, curling around her doubts and amplifying them with an insidious hiss, an echo that crawled through her bones, as if she'd swallowed something rancid that was now devouring her from the inside.

Each time it spoke, a chill settled into her spine, an icy grip that tightened until she could hardly breathe, the words scratching like claws against her sanity.

And it had been talking to her more and more lately. Gotten louder. Meaner.

Telling the truth.

Why was it inside her? She didn't know.

One thing she was certain of…the voice despised her. It wanted her dead. As the thirtieth anniversary of Clark's death crept nearer, it pulsed with an urgent hunger, growing sharper, more insistent, as if waiting for her to crumble. It gnawed at her with whispered accusations, each one colder than the last, daring her to confess—or end it before anyone could learn the truth.

Unlike so many characters living in Clarissa's head, this one wasn't especially verbose. Its words were blunt, unadorned—a voice of death that spoke with chilling clarity. At times, she almost thought of it as a twisted angel of mercy, however hideously warped that might seem.

"Memento mori." It often spoke in a foreign language. This time was especially chilling—*Remember you must die.*

Her tears doubled. Not just the occasional hot droplet, but acid streaks that burned her cheeks.

What made her hate herself more than anything was how few memories she had of her brother, other than the day she let him die. He was only seven. She couldn't remember her mother being pregnant or giving birth. Bringing a baby home from the hospital. She couldn't remember playing with him or watching him grow. Had her evil, cowardly deed erased that too?

Her parents didn't keep pictures of him displayed in their house either. Too painful, she imagined.

Clarissa closed her eyes and tried with all her might to see Clark's face. A dimple, a smile, a mop of black hair. All she ever saw were his pale hands reaching above the waves… and then nothing.

"It's over, Clarissa. It's time to end it."

The voice reverberated with a dark, unyielding force, pressing against her mind like a clamp, thick and inescapable.

"Yes." She blinked. Her vision was blurry, like she was looking through a fishbowl. She turned away from her balcony toward her apartment.

The angel of mercy sat at her patio table, cloaked in shadow. It stood, and with a whoosh of thick fabric, stepped closer. A candle burned in her living room, lending a gentle orange outline to its silhouette.

"Do it." The angel lifted its hand and pointed beyond the balcony. "Let the pain consume you. Turn around. Finish the job."

Clarissa turned back to the welcoming darkness of the sky. The letter in her hand was blackmail, but she would have to drain her retirement to meet the demand. Even then, there was no guarantee the person, whoever they were, wouldn't come back for more.

Pay for my crime or kill myself.

Death was an option…and there was something oddly comforting about that.

Clarissa stepped up to the railing and climbed over. Her bare toes gripped the ledge, her back to the railing as her sweaty hands clung tightly.

"Yes." The angel of death drew closer. "Do it. Let go. Let go, and you'll be free."

A wave of vertigo rushed over her, her own body fighting against her plans.

"We're in danger." This was a different voice, screaming from her blood, her flesh, her bones. *"Get back, move away, save yourself!"*

She closed her eyes to keep from seeing the drop from her apartment to the parking lot.

In that moment, the powerful urge to write overcame her. She wanted to go back inside, take out a notebook, and confess everything. Write out every moment she remembered of her baby brother, including the day he died, and leave it for her parents to find. Words had never failed her before.

After her death, her parents would come here, to her home. They would find the note that mentioned Clark by name. Would they understand?

They'd already lost one child. Didn't she owe them an explanation for why their surviving daughter had chosen to join him in the afterlife?

"What are you waiting for?" The angel goaded her through clenched teeth. "Do it."

She was only a child when Clark died.

"I never meant to hurt anybody."

She was surprised the words made it past the tightness in her throat, where her heartbeat pulsed with a fierce, choking rhythm.

"I never meant to fail him."

And there he was again. His small, pale hand reaching for her out of the darkness.

"I didn't mean to let them all down."

She tried to grab him, but her fingers brushed nothing more than air.

"That won't bring him back." It was the angel again, his breath warm on the back of her neck.

Clarissa sucked in a harsh breath and shook her head. The angel was right. Nothing would ever bring Clark back. Certainly not a note she had no idea how to even begin writing. What would she say? She surely couldn't detail the events of the drowning, and yet, when she thought of her only sibling, his death was the sole memory that ever surfaced. She was trapped in it. When had life gotten so cruel?

The fear of death tightened its claws around her throat.

"Yes, that's exactly what I'll do. I'll tell the truth." Words would liberate her like a caged bird taking flight. She gripped the railing tighter. "I'll tell my parents and everyone. I'll accept the consequences."

"No. They'll hate you if you tell them."

"I don't care." She sniffled and blinked away more tears. "I don't want to die, and they deserve the truth. I have to be strong."

Clarissa turned, determined to climb back over the edge.

The dark angel growled, its foul breath wrapping around her face, clogging her mouth and nostrils.

"This only works if you jump!"

"No!" Clarissa screamed as strong hands pushed her back. As her feet left the ledge, the instinct for survival kicked in, and she scrabbled for something solid. By some miracle, her fingers wrapped around the rail. She tried to hold on, but her hands were clammy.

"I've changed my mind! Help me back up." She made the mistake of looking down. Ten floors. She cried out, shrieking like a bleating lamb. "I'll tell everyone. I'll do my time!"

With a mighty heave, Clarissa hooked one arm over the railing and hauled herself up. Fueled with adrenaline, she managed to lean over the railing, half of her body back inside the safety of her balcony. Sweat poured down her face, slithered down her back. Breath rushed back into her lungs, sharp and burning. She had one last chance to live, to make things right.

"Help me, please!"

The dark angel seized her shirt, twisting the fabric in its pale hand. *Just like Clark's...*

"Thank you, thank you." Clarissa's fingers closed over an arm. "I…"

Words disappeared like whips of smoke when she looked up and into a pair of wild eyes—human eyes—right before the angel shoved her hard and gravity took hold.

Her fingers lost their grip as she tumbled backward and sank into the night. The hooded angel gazed down at her from over the balcony.

No, not an angel.

A monster.

The stars that had been smothered by the light only moments ago emerged, shimmering like distant witnesses. And there was Polaris, clearer than ever.

Beside it, other stars appeared, melding into the shape of a hand—her baby brother's. Fingers reached down from the heavens, seeking to save her.

She reached back, stretching toward him. He forgave her. She could feel it.

"Thank—"

As pain tore through her body, she knew he'd failed her, just as she had failed him so long ago.

But this time, it was okay.

2

Winter Black-Dalton clicked off a call and set her phone down next to the spicy sweet potato hash Noah had made for breakfast. Just outside the shimmering glass of her kitchen window, tiny purple blossoms were popping open on the Texas mountain laurel across the street. Spring had arrived in Austin. She wished she could smell it.

She never used to get allergies back in Richmond, but things were different here in Texas. Different flowers and grasses, a different hue to the soil. Whatever it was, she hadn't been able to breathe through her nose in a couple of days.

"What was that?" Noah sat across from her at the breakfast table, sipping his black coffee. Winter's husband had already torn through his breakfast like a pack of famished wolves were hovering behind him. Eating fast was a leftover habit from the Marines, like always arriving fifteen minutes early, a constantly swiveling head, and an odd refusal to walk on grass.

"Ariel." Sighing, Winter said her assistant's name as she propped her chin against her fist. She picked up her fork and speared a hunk of Anaheim pepper and scrambled eggs. "Looks like she's going to be out of the office for at least another two weeks."

That was no surprise, really. Only last week, a meth manufacturer held Winter's poor assistant at the end of his Desert Eagle while his deranged drug dealer girlfriend ranted about vengeance. It was Winter's fault, of course. In her work as a P.I., she'd invoked the woman's wrath by exposing the drug ring hiding behind the dealer's gold-plated makeup company.

If Winter hadn't shown up when she did, Ariel could've died. Understandably, the young woman needed time off to recover.

What worried Winter was that she might never come back.

Noah didn't say anything. He was squinting out the window with a little grin on his face, watching the season's first hummingbird imbibe from the feeder he'd put out. He really had a knack for all this homemaking stuff—gardening, cooking. He even knew how to work an iron like a wizard. Winter hadn't known that side of him when she'd married her husband, but it was definitely a perk.

But as her words had time to sink in, he reached for her hand. "I don't like the idea of you being alone at the office."

She grunted in agreement. "I don't especially like it, either, but that's the way the cookie crumbles."

"I'll come by after I'm done with Falkner."

Noah's boss at the Violent Crimes Unit had scheduled him for an exit interview before he officially went on his one-year sabbatical. Today would be his last as an active-duty FBI agent.

Winter understood how badly he needed a break, even if she still had questions that she mostly kept to herself. In the last few months, even before moving to Austin, she'd noticed a change in her no-nonsense, tough-as-nails husband.

Neither of them had been the same after her brother reappeared in her life, leaving her with psychological scars no therapist could heal. And the experience made Noah more anxious, more cautious, more pensive. He had no problem risking his life on the regular, but it was different when it was his wife in danger.

Winter knew this. She could feel it whenever he looked at her. She'd tried every way she knew of to convince him not to worry, but telling him for the umpteenth time that she could handle herself wouldn't soothe his deep-seated anxiety.

Maybe the sabbatical would change that. Maybe without the pressure of the job, he'd be able to process what had happened and come back stronger. In the meantime…

"I don't think it's wise for you to just hop right into work." At last, Winter took a bite of her breakfast. "This is a unique opportunity. I want you to spend a while just relaxing and figuring out what makes you happy. Maybe there's something out there other than the FBI. You deserve the time to discover that."

Noah shook his head, like she knew he would. "There's still someone out there who wants to hurt you. Someone who's been watching you."

His words were like spiders crawling up her neck. A few weeks ago, Noah and Winter had noticed that someone had installed remote cameras outside her grandparents' home and her office, piggybacking on local Wi-Fi to broadcast back to some unknown location. When Noah tracked down the offender, Carl Gardner, they'd learned he wasn't working alone.

The whole thing was still up in the air. They were no closer to identifying whoever had sent Gardner than they had been at the start. When federal agents had come to apprehend him Gardner had taken shots at them, so Noah had no choice but to put the asshole down. He died before medical help arrived, taking all his secrets with him. Still, evidence on his many computers hinted at the motivation behind all the illegal surveillance.

Someone—a puppet master pulling Gardner's strings—was stalking Winter.

To make it all worse, her was a member of Justin Black's fan community. Justin. Winter's little brother. The infamous serial killer. The man who kidnapped, drugged, and tortured her. Who threatened children to make her do unspeakable things. Laughing all the while at the chaos and horror as his sadistic mind schemed up more and more ways to cause misery.

Winter didn't like to think about the people out there in the world who adored Justin as some kind of idol—women who sent him naked photos and proposed, men who modeled themselves after him. Any face she saw in a crowd might be one of them.

Her stalker had been making it his mission to finish the work Justin started before Winter delivered him to federal authorities, ensuring he'd be incarcerated in an undisclosed supermax prison for the rest of his life.

The whole thing—especially the not knowing—left Winter feeling helpless and weak. She'd rather have an actual spider crawling up her neck than feel that way.

Noah stood and walked to the counter to refill his mug. "The security cameras I ordered are supposed to arrive at your office today. When I'm done with Falkner, I'll come by and install them."

She wanted to argue. His anxiety was more contagious than a cold, and that was all she needed when her nose was already stuffed. "Kline called and said he was feeling better. He's supposed to be in today. I'm sure he can handle it."

Two days ago, Kline had flown in from Philadelphia to tell her he knew why his sister had died. He got as far as, *"Brace yourself. You're really not going to like it,"* before he ran to the bathroom and started throwing up.

She hadn't seen him since.

Noah looked consummately unimpressed. It wasn't that he didn't like Kline Hurst, which was the name they still called her recently discovered biological father. Well, it wasn't only that.

Winter heaved a sigh. "What?"

"You really think Kline's your man for setting up a complex, interconnected Wi-Fi security system?"

She nearly smiled. "Are you saying he's incompetent?"

"Of course not. He can swing a hammer like nobody's business. But he's old. Real old."

"He's not that old." Winter rolled her eyes. "Fine. You can come set up the system. He can mount the gadgets, though. But I really don't want you to feel obligated to come work for me."

His eyebrow shot up. *"For* you?"

She smiled. *"With* me. It's just…I know you've been on the FBI path most of your life, even when you were in the service. This is the first time you've had a chance to really look around and decide. Do you even want to be in law enforcement anymore, or would you rather open a restaurant?"

The eyebrow went even higher. "A restaurant?"

"That's just an example. I'm just saying, this sabbatical is supposed to be about you, not about me. You should take some time to get to know yourself." She spread her arms wide. "The world is your oyster."

The eyebrow sank into a frown. "I thought you

needed me."

His big green eyes sparkled, drawing her in even from across the room. Winter's heart went all squishy, like it only ever did for him.

"Of course I need you."

"You don't want me cramping your style, is that it?"

Her heart wanted Noah with her every second of the day, but that wasn't how normal, healthy relationships worked. "I have no style." She laughed and shook her head. "You're always welcome at Black Investigations. I told you that already. But I can't afford to pay you what you're worth. I can't afford to pay you, well, anything."

"It's gonna be all right, darlin'. We have savings, I'll be getting a third of my salary, and I have every intention of making more money on the side."

She rolled her eyes. "All the more reason to take a few days to figure out how you want to do that. Besides, I thought you had all these grand plans for the back garden?"

"It'd be nice to get out in the garden." He looked wistfully out the window like a sailor viewing the sea. "Once the cameras are in. And Ariel's back. Maybe. If I feel like it."

A pang that felt an awful lot like guilt stabbed through Winter's stomach. She loved that he was so invested in keeping her safe—she never could've loved someone who felt differently. At the same time, she wondered if he was stifling himself for her sake.

"Speaking of work, I better get going." After screwing the travel top onto his coffee mug, Noah slung his laptop bag over his shoulder, approached Winter, and pecked her lips.

"What does Falkner want with you anyway?"

"I gotta turn in my reports on the trafficking bust, and he wants to do an exit interview."

"Sounds fun." Winter returned his kiss with a groan. Noah had done nothing but complain about his boss since day one at the Austin office. The man had become the little avatar on his shoulder, just like Darnell was on hers, harping in her ear. Who would he have with Falkner no longer there?

"I dunno." Noah shrugged. "It might be okay. Falkner isn't a bad guy. I was just mad at him, because…well, because he was right about me."

"Good luck, baby." Winter patted her husband's butt. "I'll see you soon."

As she watched him leave, she wondered what he'd choose to do over the next year. If he'd even go back to the FBI when the year was over. It'd be incredible if he decided to join her in the private sector full time, but she didn't want him to do that from a sense of obligation.

If Noah were to become her partner again—like when she still worked for the Bureau—it should be because he wanted to, not because he worried she might get herself killed if he wasn't watching her back.

For Noah's sake, Winter needed to keep out of trouble. Give him a break from constantly worrying about her, so he could worry about himself and move toward what made him happy and fulfilled.

But trouble always had a way of finding her.

3

Winter searched a local news website on her phone and let the stories stream in the background as she cleared the dishes and started the dishwasher. There was talk about the road construction that forced her to take the longer, slower way downtown and how it was probably going to take at least six months longer than originally projected because of sewer lines and blah, blah, blah.

"Dammit." She picked up the metal scrubber that looked like a chunk of chainmail and scrubbed the bottom of a cast-iron skillet she'd given Noah on his last birthday. He sure loved cooking in it, but she always seemed to be the one left cleaning up the mess.

"In other news, readers are mourning the death of children's author Clarissa Toler, who was found dead early this morning in a case of apparent suicide. Her most famous books, The Fairies of Eastwind, *are beloved by children the world over and are in series development for the streaming service—"*

Winter scrolled down to check the weather, pausing the video. More rain in the forecast.

When she and Noah first decided to move to Texas, she'd had visions of old westerns, where the land was all dry and barren, covered with sagebrush and cactuses. She certainly hadn't expected to wear rain boots almost every day, but that was the way spring had been treating her so far. The greenery all through the city suggested this would be a regular thing.

She needed a shower before work, so after starting the dishwasher, she turned on some music and headed to the bathroom, where she stripped down to her birthday suit. As she was about to step into the steam, her phone rang. The ID read *Austin Police Department*, but it wasn't a number she recognized.

"This is Winter Black." She grabbed a towel and wrapped it around herself, as though the caller could somehow see her.

"Hello, Ms. Black. My name is Detective Harlan Lessner. I need you to come down to the station and answer a few questions."

"What's this about?"

"One of your advertising flyers was found at a crime scene this morning."

"Advertising flyers?" Winter and Ariel had talked about running some advertisements if word-of-mouth business ever dried up, but that time hadn't yet come.

Ariel wouldn't have sent out flyers without asking her to sign off on them first. Then again, Ariel had been getting more and more frazzled right before everything came to a head with her hostage situation.

"I don't understand. What scene? What is this in connection to?"

"I'll be happy to explain more in person. Can you make it down this morning, please?"

"Yeah, sure. I just need to get ready, then I'll head that way."

"Thank you, Ms. Black." The line went dead.

Winter stared at her phone a moment before shooting Ariel a quick text. She rehung the towel she'd needlessly wrapped herself in and put her hair up to keep it from getting wet. Just as she was about to step into the shower, her phone buzzed.

Ariel.

I never sent out any flyers, but I mocked up a few designs. I could finish that while I'm at home if you want.

The message made Winter smile. It was the first real indication Ariel planned to return to work.

She didn't want to read into it, though. Her feelings on the matter were immaterial. Her only job was to give Ariel the space and time she needed to make up her own mind.

She texted back, telling her not to worry about it. Then she set down her phone and stepped into the steamy water.

※

Detective Harlan Lessner was in his forties, with tan skin and a crescent of black hair framing his mostly bald head. His body was squat and rounded, his head bulbous—a bit like Danny DeVito, but half a foot taller and with a toothbrush mustache. He'd worked with the Austin PD for a few years, but with hundreds of officers on the force, it was no surprise he and Winter had never met.

They sat together in the interview room, Winter trying to suck all the warmth from the mocha latte she'd bought at a drive-through on the way over. She'd been in a lot of these rooms, all over the country, and they were always frigid. It was intentional, of course, a way to increase anxiety and get people to talk just so they could get out of the miserable little icebox.

Lessner took out an evidence bag with a single sheet of paper inside and set it on the table in front of Winter. It was folded in thirds, as if it had been stuffed inside an envelope. Even if she hadn't heard back from Ariel, the moment Winter saw the spartan design, she knew her vivacious assistant had nothing to do with it.

The page was white with Courier New typeface. *Black Investigations* was set across the top, followed by the address and phone number. No logo, no slogan. It looked like something a high school business teacher would point to as an example of bad advertising.

She gazed across the table at the detective. "This didn't come from my office. I've never seen it before."

Lessner pressed his lips together, eyeing the paper. "Are you absolutely certain?"

"One-hundred-percent. I've never done any advertising. I rely on word of mouth." She turned the paper over to find a blank page. "Where'd you find this?"

"On Clarissa Toler's tenth-floor balcony. Do you know her?"

The name was familiar. The dots connected.

"No. But I heard the name on the news this morning."

"She died. An apparent suicide. Leaped over her balcony around one this morning." Lessner tilted his head. "Do you have any idea why somebody would want to make or distribute advertisements for your business?"

Winter thought for a moment. "I was in the FBI for years, and now I'm a P.I., so there's no shortage of people who dislike me. But this is strange. I'm sorry, but I have no idea."

"Why don't you take a bit of time and think about it?" Lessner reached into his jacket pocket and took out a business card, which he slid across the table to her. "If you have any thoughts, anything at all, please contact me right away."

Nodding, Winter picked up the card and looked at it, like she knew she was supposed to. "No problem, though Darnell Davenport is my usual contact."

"Detective Davenport was subpoenaed to testify in a case in New Mexico. He won't be back for another few days. Maybe longer, depending."

Lucky Darnell. Bet it isn't raining in New Mexico.

Winter nodded. "I don't understand why my flyer would be significant, forged or otherwise. Clarissa's death is a suicide, right?"

He completely ignored the question. "Thank you for taking the time to come speak with me. I'll be in contact if we need anything more."

Winter sighed and put the card in her pocket as she rose from her seat. Why did she ever bother asking cops anything? They never answered. And even when they did, it was never a clear answer.

Then again, she was certain she did exactly the same thing when people asked her inconvenient questions. She had no right to complain, and yet it never ceased to irritate her.

Detective Lessner shook her hand and led her out of the station. As she walked toward her car, her nose dribbling with allergies, she got a strange, familiar chill that someone was watching her.

But the parking lot was open and empty, not a soul in sight.

It was a very strange thing for a third party to put out advertisements for a business without consent or permission. In all her years in this work, she'd never heard of such a thing and was having a hard time coming up with any possible motive for the action.

But Winter didn't want to stand in this lot wondering about it anymore while phantom eyes burned into her back. With a confused sigh, she got into her SUV and headed to her office.

4

Winter slid her key in the lock of her office door and keyed in her code. The double lock system had been Noah's idea, a way to try to keep her safe. She certainly didn't mind it.

Walking into the empty office, she had to fight to keep herself from feeling disappointed. Kline had promised to be there that morning so they could finish their talk from two days before. Of course, he'd also said that yesterday. By this point, she knew to take everything he said with a grain of salt.

Until recently, her biological father had been nothing more than a line in her late mother's diary. He'd proven no less elusive in person—here one moment and gone the next. There was so much she wanted to talk to him about. At the same time, she never had any idea what to say. Everything about the relationship was confusing and uncomfortable.

On the other hand, Kline had done a bang-up job acting as Freddy Fix-It around the office. He'd polished the floors, so desperately needed after last week's double homicide had stained the blond oak floorboards he'd just finished sealing two months ago. He also fixed the plumbing in the break room. A few things still required attention, especially the leaky toilet and ancient air-conditioning unit, but Kline had promised to get around to those soon. And then…what?

She had no idea what to do with him when the work was done. Was she supposed to keep him on as an employee? Was she supposed to help him find other work? What, if any, obligations did she have toward the man who provided half her DNA before making an untold number of questionable decisions for the past three decades?

The little bell attached to the door rang.

"Excuse me."

Winter flinched and whirled around. She hated how easily she'd startled, hated how fast her pulse was. One hand flew to her hip, where an FBI-issue sidearm used to hang in its holster.

The man stepping through her door seemed innocuous enough, but she never trusted anything so superficial as appearances. He wore a khaki raincoat, and an umbrella hung unopened in one hand. His hair was so blond it almost looked white, and his eyes were green as cut grass. His skin was tan and smooth with rounded cheekbones and a square jaw. A Ken doll come to life.

The weight of the gun holstered around her left ankle grew heavier. When she first left the Bureau, she'd hoped to set aside firearms in favor of more peaceful tools, but violence and trouble still plagued her everywhere she went. She'd decided to keep a small .38 Special revolver on her person for the foreseeable future. Just in case.

It had come in handy when Winter found herself at the mercy of a murderous drug manufacturer and his two shotgun-wielding sons on her previous case. If not for her little sidearm, her brains would've been spattered all over the back deck of that run-down meth house out in the middle of nowhere.

Winter smiled politely at the man. "Can I help you?"

"I got your flyer. I need your help."

Her interest flared with a physical twinge in her shoulders. She flicked on the lights in the office. "Come on in. I'm Winter Black. Did you bring the flyer with you, by chance?"

Please, say yes. I'd like to do my own DNA analysis. Something tells me my fairy godmother didn't fashion these on her magic sewing machine and deliver them on a flying carpet.

"I think so. I'm Perry. It's nice to meet you."

Winter walked past the man, locked her front door—she'd do that from now on—and gestured him forward with a wave. When she turned to face him, he reached toward his back pocket. On instinct again, Winter's hand went to her hip again, but she casually turned the motion into a scratch when Perry pulled out a white piece of paper.

The paper was folded in thirds and then in half, creases stained blue from his dark jeans. He unfolded it and held it out to her.

Winter didn't take it. There might yet be fingerprints or other trace evidence on the paper, so the less it was handled, the better.

As Perry watched her with wide eyes, she walked to her desk, put on a latex glove, and grabbed an evidence bag for the paper. Once it was safely stored and sealed, she snapped off her glove and narrowed her gaze at the flyer. She couldn't think of a worse, more pedestrian font, especially for advertising. A criminal's bad taste, however, was not the issue. With the paper in her hand, her anger rose.

No red glow, though.

Unsurprisingly, it was exactly the same flyer as the one Lessner showed her. "Where'd you get this?"

The man shrugged. "It was in my mailbox."

"Was it in an envelope?"

His face creased in thought. "I don't think so. No."

Based on the tripart folds on this flyer and the one Lessner showed her, she'd assumed someone had stamped and mailed them. She turned the evidence bag over in her hands. No address written on the back, no postage on the paper. Someone must have delivered it by hand.

Technically, it was illegal for anything without a stamp to go in a USPS mailbox. She wondered why the person who'd made the flyers would risk being seen versus just sending them through a postal service.

Likely, so the mail couldn't be traced.

Winter moved to her desk and dropped the bagged paper onto the surface. She motioned for Perry to sit as she settled into her own chair.

Perry looked terribly uncomfortable, his spine rigid, his feet flat on the floor, his hands fidgeting.

She flipped a notepad to a fresh page. "How can I help you, Perry…?"

"Perry Bick. I'm being blackmailed."

Another twinge of interest ran down Winter's spine. She leaned back in her seat. "I'm listening."

He reached into his pocket, and again, she tensed until he took out another piece of folded paper, this time hesitating before passing it over.

Winter put on fresh gloves and unfolded the paper. Trifold, just like the flyer, and typed, though with a different font. Sans serif and narrow. A few scant sentences.

Before she read a word, her eyes were immediately drawn to a smudge mark in one corner. "What's this?"

"Mine." Perry kept his eyes on his knees. "I was eating. Sorry."

Internally sighing with disappointment, Winter read the paper out loud. "'You know what you did, and so do I. You will initiate three transfers of $10,000 each for three consecutive days to the following Paymo account. Failure to complete any of these transfers will result in revealing your secret publicly. Alternatively, you can kill yourself. The truth will die with you. The choice is yours.'" Winter raised an eyebrow at the sign-off. "'The Listener.'"

At the bottom of the paper was an email address—a random stream of letters and numbers at some private server she'd never heard of, all the information Perry would need to transfer his money to the blackmailer.

She silently read the letter a second time as her brow furrowed with confusion. "It's very unusual."

"What do you mean?"

"I've known people to end their lives to avoid blackmail, but I've never known a blackmailer to offer it as an option."

Perry twisted his fingers in his lap. "The letter came the same day your flyer did. I thought you might know something about it."

She shook her head. She considered mentioning that the flyer hadn't come from her office, but she held back. Perhaps Perry Bick was the one sending out the fake ads, and this whole blackmail thing was just for show. For all she knew, Clarissa Toler didn't commit suicide, and she'd received the same blackmail threat along with Winter's fake flyer.

Except she'd taken option two.

Unless she hadn't.

Winter bit her lip. Perry Bick could be in danger. Or he could be the criminal behind these threats. It wouldn't be the first time she was face-to-face with the engineer behind criminal activity. They seemed to be drawn to her like flies to honey. She had to play this safe until this man left her office.

"I'm guessing this didn't come with a stamp either?"

Perry shook his head.

"I'm guessing you know what the secret is that the letter refers to?"

His face darkened, which was more than enough of an answer.

"Did you just come here to ask about the flyer, or are you looking for someone to help you with this?"

Perry hunched his shoulders. "I looked you up online. You seem legit."

Gee.

"Would you help me?"

"First things first. I need to know what we're dealing with here." Winter tapped the letter with her forefinger. "What are you being blackmailed for?"

"Something that happened a really long time ago. It doesn't really matter."

Winter pressed her lips into a thin line. "If you want my help, you have to be honest with me. A smart man never lies to his doctor, his divorce lawyer, or his P.I."

Perry looked like he was in physical pain, but he blew out his cheeks and nodded. "Okay, but this is just between us. You can't tell anybody, including the police."

"I'm bound by confidentiality. If you are my client, I cannot disclose that or any other information you share with me except where I am required by law." She waved her hand toward the framed certificate on the wall behind her. "Doing so could jeopardize my license."

Winter hoped that was a good enough answer, since he wasn't technically her client yet.

"All right. Fine." Perry rubbed his hands over his face and hair and sucked a deep inhale through his nose.

Winter sniffled, feeling vaguely jealous of his functioning sinuses.

"When I was in college, I worked at a strip club." He paused, his breathing heavy.

"That's it?" Winter raised an eyebrow. "That's not so bad.

Unless you're a priest now or something. Definitely not worth thirty grand."

"No, that's not it. I…dammit."

"It's okay. Take your time."

He slammed his fist rhythmically against his knee. "I went to EKU, Eastern Kentucky University. So you got a lot of, uh… I don't what you would call them. Braindead redneck assholes."

"Okay."

"Yeah, so the club I worked at. Women went there, but it was also kind of a gay club. There were a lot of guys in the audience. And that was fine." Perry held his hands up in front of him. "Like, I don't care. Sometimes, you'd get one that was really drunk and handsy, but mostly everyone was polite and tipped really well. It was a great job. I made bank. I mean, my student loans are paid off. You know what I'm saying?"

"Got you."

"But so, there was this liquor store next door." Perry dropped his hands back into his lap and started twisting his fingers again. "One night, this guy from my school saw me leaving work. He followed me to my car. He was harassing me, calling me all sorts of homophobic shit. He took my bag and poured it out and found my, um, costume. And he was saying how he was going to tell everyone at school, everyone in the town that I was, like, a gay sex worker."

"And…?"

Perry rubbed his temple. "If we were in Austin, it wouldn't have mattered, but where I was living in the dorms…I mean, he was going to make my life a living hell."

Winter leaned back in her chair and cupped her chin in her hand. She was starting to get a bad feeling about where this was going.

"He kept calling me names. He wouldn't let me leave. Then he spat in my face, and I just lost it." His voice dropped low. "I kicked the shit out of him. I mean, I don't even remember it that well. I snapped. And when I kinda came back to myself, he was bleeding a lot and unconscious. I left him there in the parking lot all alone. I just left him."

"What happened to him?"

"The next day, I found out he was in a coma."

Winter took a sip of her coffee. It was stone cold.

Perry looked like he was going to throw up. She wanted to offer him water, but feared if she did, she'd miss the conclusion of this tale.

"He's still in a coma," he finally said. "He never woke up."

That was quite the secret to carry through life. "So he was never able to tell anybody what happened?"

Perry shook his head, face turned toward the floor. She thought she saw tears glistening on his eyelashes.

"Have you ever told anybody?"

Again, he shook his head.

"So somebody must've seen you that night?"

"That's what I've been trying to figure out. It was dark and empty. Nobody was around, I remember that. I would've noticed. I don't know. It all feels like a dream. Like something that happened to somebody else." He met Winter's eyes. "I'm not a violent person. That's the only time I ever hurt anybody."

"It's always in your best interest not to capitulate to blackmailers, but what you've just confessed to is very serious."

Perry's face darkened, his gaze falling back to the floor.

"When exactly did this take place?"

"Seventeen years ago. I don't remember the date, but it was winter, a couple weeks before Christmas."

He was just a kid. Winter massaged the ridge above her eyes. *Just a dumb kid.* "You say the crime took place in Kentucky. Which county?"

"Madison." His voice had grown so soft, barely above a whisper.

"Can you tell me the man's name?"

He shook his head. "I don't know it."

Though she kept her expression neutral, Winter's mind raced. How could Perry know the victim's condition but not his name? It would've been in the news.

Perry's story had some holes in it, yet his teary eyes spoke to genuine grief. He'd clearly spent years punishing himself, ruminating on what might happen should anybody find out. At the same time, most people who were capable of empathy and regret—and who got away with such a heinous crime—wanted to be caught on some level. Though the prospect of punishment was frightening, it offered guilty people a way to cleanse their conscience.

Before she took this man as a client, she needed some facts to work with.

Winter woke up her laptop and quickly searched the statute of limitations on aggravated assault in the state of Kentucky. If the crime had taken place in Texas, Perry would've been in the clear, as it was considered a misdemeanor and he was far beyond the statute of limitations. Kentucky, on the other hand, would likely consider aggravated assault a felony in his case, and there was no time limitation placed on any felony within their borders.

She didn't want to cause a scene. The path of least resistance was always the best option in cases like this. "Will you excuse me for a moment? I'll be right back."

"Okay." Perry slumped in his chair. He looked utterly defeated, as though finally confessing his secret had drained the life out of him.

Winter swiped her phone off the desk and stepped out, closing her office door behind her. Heading to the back where she could still keep an eye on him, she found the Madison County Sheriff's Office number.

She had questions, and if Perry wouldn't answer them, she'd try another way.

The phone rang three times, and she was forced to contend with an automated touchtone system before an actual human picked up the line. Winter explained her situation to the officer and was transferred. She had to explain two more times before she was connected with a detective in the Madison County Violent Crimes Unit.

"You got Detective Schiller." Her voice was brusque and raspy against the background sounds of a busy office—muffled conversation, beeping phones, the cadence of footsteps on tile.

"My name is Winter Black. I'm a private investigator in Austin, Texas. I've received a tip regarding an aggravated assault cold case that took place in your county seventeen years ago."

Winter ran down the few details she had. The location outside of a strip club, the victim ending up in a coma. Schiller listened, fingers tapping on a keyboard, and asked follow-up questions Winter didn't have answers for. The detective put her on hold while she looked up the case.

Shuffling on her feet, Winter kept her attention on her office. She could just see the top of Perry's head through the glass walls. He was still sitting in his chair, his head bowed.

The line clicked over, and Detective Schiller came back on. "You sure this was in Madison County?"

"Yes."

"I don't have any unsolved AAs or SBIs matching any of your description. Could the date be wrong?"

Winter was confused. "I'm not sure why this source would share the crime with me if he wasn't telling the truth."

"You'd be surprised what people will do for attention."

Winter almost snorted. It took a hell of a lot more than that to surprise her.

"Gimme another sec." Again, the phone clicked. This time, Schiller left her on hold for nearly ten minutes with some skippy hold music bebopping in her ear. All the while, Winter kept peeking to make sure Perry wasn't trying to leave.

He hadn't so much as shifted in his chair. Perry seemed like a smart enough man. He had to suspect that she was double checking his story—might even be thinking that she was turning him in, which only supported her theory that he was ready to be punished. Ready for the nightmare of his own guilt to come to an end.

It very well might come to that, but not this minute.

"I did a pull on the whole Bluegrass Region for the entire month of December, and I got nothing."

What the hell? "Are you sure?"

"Sure as the day follows the night. Either your source has a shoddy memory, or they're nuts. Take your pick." Winter heard the rustle of papers over the line. "I got your number. If anything comes up, I'll let you know. But don't hold your breath."

"But what should I do about my source?"

"Do whatever the hell you want. Have a nice day." The line went dead.

Winter looked down at the black screen of her phone as if she were waiting for it to do something more. When it didn't, she slipped it into her pocket and walked back to her office.

Perry flinched as she stepped inside, his big green eyes gazing up like a puppy who just peed on the carpet.

The chair creaked as she lowered herself into it. She went into a desk drawer and pulled out one of the premade folders of new client paperwork Ariel had put together. She tossed it onto the table in front of him. "I'll take the job."

"What? You will?" He stared at her. The man was so handsome and hopeful, it was almost hard to look directly at him. "Thank you. Thank you so much. When I saw your flyer in the mail, I thought it was like the universe sending me a message, telling me to contact you. I just knew you'd be my way out of this mess."

"Don't get ahead of yourself, but I love a good puzzle. I'll do my best to solve it."

Perry took the folder and stood to leave. Winter held her hand up to stop him.

"I need you to do something. I know it's hard, but it'd be extremely helpful if you could write down all the details you remember from that night. Every little thing, even if you think it's unimportant. The day, the date, the name of the club, the name of the liquor store. Cross streets. Sensory details, who you saw before and after, the name of the hospital where the man is, or was initially, in the coma. Can you do that?"

He nodded. "I'll try."

"Include secondary sources too. Do you think you knew his name at one point, but trauma erased it?" She gave him a small smile. "Our memories do funny things. Anything you can think of might help us figure out who else could've known what happened and lead us to the blackmailer."

Perry clutched the paperwork to his chest. "That makes sense."

"And why was it, do you think, this blackmailer waited seventeen years to contact you? Could it be someone you knew from back then? Waiting this long suggests it could be someone from that time."

"I hear what you're saying, and it's all I've been thinking

about lately, but I don't know if I can answer any of those questions."

Winter rose to shake his hand. "Well, you need to try."

After the door closed, she watched until Perry disappeared down the sidewalk and around a corner. Either he was a superb actor, or his story had to be true on some level. Maybe he'd gotten his dates confused. Or the place.

As perplexed as she was over the wild situation with Perry, Winter's mind quickly circled back to the other detail. The flyer for her own office that had accompanied the blackmail demand.

Clearly, this part of the message was for her, not anyone else. Unfortunately, she still had no idea what any of it meant. Clarissa Toler was dead, so getting straight answers out of her would be impossible. Still, she wondered what else Perry Bick and Clarissa Toler had in common. If she could find the connection, it could lead her straight to the person putting out the flyers, who was likely the blackmailer too.

Detective Lessner hadn't said anything about the children's book author being blackmailed. Then again, he hadn't said much of anything. Was it possible a letter just like the one Perry received had pushed Clarissa to take her own life?

For now, her best lead was Perry Bick. If only she could figure out which parts of what he'd told her were actually true.

5

Noah stood rigidly in front of SSA Falkner's desk, arms to his side and chin up. At attention, as he had been for so much of his career.

The older man was no less stiff-backed in his office chair, but there was something almost lazy in the tilt of his chin and the stroke of his blue pen as he scanned the papers on his desk. He didn't make a mark on any of them, though his hand was always at the ready.

That was Weston Falkner in a nutshell. Vigilant, intelligent, and very good at his job. But there was another side to him Noah had glimpsed only recently, when preparing to leave for his sabbatical. Prior to that, Falkner had loomed before him like a disappointed disciplinarian. Since then, he'd become more of a human being.

"Everything seems to be in order." He closed his fountain pen and put it back in his top pocket. He always used the same pen, drank from the same plain white mug, and wore the same three suits—gray, grayer, and slightly less gray. High quality and practical all at once. "I'd say I was disappointed you left the scene so quickly, but there's really no point, is there?"

Noah's jaw tightened. "My wife was in danger. I didn't have a choice."

"I understand. You were both witness to a murder-suicide in her office that very day. I hope the cleanup team I recommended did good work."

"Yes, thank you. They were excellent. We had to replace some furniture, and Winter got unreasonably excited about installing a clear refrigerator for water bottles in the client area, but otherwise, the place is just the same as before… though I don't know if it's ever been that clean."

"I'm glad to hear it." Falkner closed the folder in front of him and placed it into a rack of seven holders stacked on a table behind his desk. "You did a thorough job on your exit forms, so I don't have any further questions. Was there anything you wanted to ask me?"

Noah blinked. He did have a question he wanted to ask, but he worried it might be too personal for the setting. But if he didn't ask now, he might never get another opportunity.

The rash that had been spreading across his back for going on three weeks now—the doctor said it was stress hives—had been getting better ever since he made peace with his unplanned sabbatical. Still, as he mulled over whether to speak or forever hold his peace, he felt the old, familiar itch on his shoulder blade.

"May I ask you a personal question, sir?"

Falkner stiffened and looked at his watch. Then he gestured toward the chair in front of his desk, silently inviting Noah to sit. "I have a few minutes."

"Thank you." Noah took a seat, setting his hands lightly on each knee. "You mentioned before that you took a sabbatical once. I was just curious what you did with your time."

The shadow of a rare smile drifted across his colorless lips, but it died before it touched his eyes. "I've taken two. The first was after my wife and I split. I lived in Morocco for a time."

"Morocco? Why?"

He shrugged, his spine loosening. "I've seen *Casablanca* one too many times."

Noah grinned. "I love that movie."

"Really? Most people haven't actually seen it. Just Bugs Bunny making fun of it."

"So what did you do while you were there?"

"I read a lot of books, drank too much, seriously considered buying a monkey." Falkner's lips curved up. "I volunteered here and there in a library near where I lived. Mostly, I thought about all the mistakes I made that had landed me there. And everything I'd been through that I'd spent the last decade not thinking about while it was actually happening to me."

Noah felt strange sitting there listening to him, like he'd just been invited into somebody's home. Not the place where they lived, but the place they came from.

"I was about your age then," Falkner continued, "maybe a little older. My daughters were just starting high school. I have twins, by the way."

"You had kids in high school when you were my age?" Noah balked. "How old do you think I am?"

"I got my ex-wife pregnant when we were seventeen, so…"

Noah's eyes widened, and he shook his head. "I can't even imagine that."

"We got married right away, like people did back then." Falkner shrugged one shoulder. "But I was on deployment by the time they were born. I didn't even meet them 'til they were almost six months old. She mostly raised them by herself."

"So you took a sabbatical to deal with your divorce?"

"My ex-wife met someone and was engaged before I could blink. My daughters were crazy about him and so into the wedding and getting their bridesmaid dresses that I felt superfluous in the whole equation. He was their judo sensei, had been for years before he married my ex."

Noah winced. "Ouch."

Falkner rubbed his hand over the back of his neck. "It took me that whole year to come to terms with just how grateful I should've been to that man for stepping up when I was too busy at work to be a father or a husband. My daughters are the strong, confident, well-adjusted women they are today because of him."

Noah had not expected such an intimate answer from a man he didn't even like. "Sir. I didn't mean to pry—"

"If I'd taken sabbatical a year earlier, before Vanessa divorced me, my life could've been very different." Falkner dropped his hand and pressed his palm flat on the desk. "I had to lose her, my children, and my self-respect before I realized there was more to life than the Bureau. Then again, if it hadn't happened, I never would've gone to Morocco. I never would've met Damiya, the woman I've been lucky enough to call my wife for going on twenty years."

Noah smiled. He hadn't expected the story to have a happy ending. "That's terrific."

"I admire how devoted you are to your wife. You two are lucky to have each other. This is a hard life you've chosen, both of you." Falkner jabbed his finger at Noah. "You end up keeping secrets in this job, whether you want to or not. Secrets that'll rip you apart if you don't have somebody at home who you trust and who trusts you back. Take it from someone who's been there. Treat your marriage like the fragile gift it is, or it'll break, and you'll be left looking at the pieces, wondering what the hell happened."

Each of his words landed as gently as feathers, but the cumulative effect was as heavy as a lead weight.

That was exactly why Noah was taking this sabbatical—because Winter meant more to him than any job ever could.

Noah swallowed. "You said you took another sabbatical?"

"In other countries, they'd just call it parental leave. When my son was born." Falkner smiled and flipped around a picture sitting on his desk so Noah could see. In it, two identical pale women with blond hair stood posing with a dark-skinned young man. All three of them were tall and thin and had their father's aquiline nose and serious eyes.

A thorn twisted painfully in Noah's swelling heart, a feeling that had become more and more familiar over the last few months, though he wasn't sure why. He was scared to probe himself too deeply, not knowing what he might find in the twisted patch of briars his brain was turning into. "You have a beautiful family."

"Thank you." He flipped the picture back, his eyes lingering on it for a moment before meeting Noah's. "Have you and Winter ever thought of starting a family?"

"I…" Noah cleared his throat. "We've never really talked about it."

"Well, this next year will be a good time to have all those conversations, with yourself at the very least." The fluorescent light caught the hint of a twinkle in his eyes. "And don't wait too long. Have your children young enough that you'll be alive to play with your grandchildren."

"You're a grandpa?"

"I'm about to be." Falkner smiled—a real smile with teeth and everything. "Cheryl's due in August."

"Congratulations."

"Thank you." Checking his watch again, Falkner stood and extended his hand for a shake. "Good luck, Dalton. I scheduled a final official debriefing for you in fifteen minutes, so you can head on down and wait for them. Then you're out of here."

"Thank you, sir."

Falkner cocked his head. "In spite of what every single agent seems to think about themselves, the Bureau's going to be just fine without you." He paused, a whisper of a boyish smile brushing his faded cheeks. "But don't worry. The FBI will be here when you're ready to come back."

Noah left Weston Falkner's office knowing there was a good chance he'd probably never see or speak to the man ever again. If someone had asked him about that two weeks ago, he'd have said he was damn glad of it. Now he couldn't help but feel melancholy.

Their conversation fluttered through his brain even as butterflies flapped in his stomach. He sensed this wasn't the end. He'd be back in a year, back at his desk as if nothing had changed.

Unless, of course, he wasn't. Only then did it fully hit him that today might be his last day as a federal agent, his last time in this building. Other than being closer to Winter, he had no idea what he was going to do with himself. His life was wide open. No schedule, no time constraints, no lofty goals looming ahead. For the first time in his life, he was truly directionless.

It was liberating. And terrifying.

As he waited in the hall for his final debriefing, Noah found his thoughts wandering in a confused and muddled way, slowly snaking back toward grandchildren. He imagined himself as an old man out in the garden at his and Winter's Destiny Bluff home with cute little humans sitting in the strawberry patch, smearing their faces with red juice and smiling in the sun.

It suddenly crystalized in his brain that he wanted to be a grandpa someday. And that meant he wanted to be a father.

He'd always ascribed to the arguably sexist notion that only women had biological clocks. But in that moment, Noah's own clock wound to life and started ticking.

6

Kline came in nearly three hours later than Winter expected him, smelling of cigarettes and looking frazzled and tired. Every time she tried to ask him to sit down to finish their conversation from two days before, he'd made some excuse to put it off.

Though she was itching to know what he knew about his sister's death, she also knew the man well enough to realize he would share the story when he was good and ready.

"I've found out more about Opal and how she died. I mean, why she died. Brace yourself. You're really not going to like it."

Then…vomit.

Though he looked some better, he clearly wasn't ready to finish the story. Dammit.

After tinkering with the toilet, he told her the air conditioner parts would likely take another week to be delivered, since that contraption was old. Winter was glad it was still April, though any month in Texas was hotter than she liked.

"I have everything prepped, so it's just a matter of

snapping the condenser into place. I bet your man could probably even handle that."

Winter smiled and thanked him for his efforts, but then they stood there as seconds slid past in silence. Was he ready to tell her now?

Nope.

Instead, he'd asked her what he needed to do next. Which was a problem. He'd finished all the repairs she had available for him, which brought the issue she'd been contemplating for a while into sharp relief.

What was she supposed to do with him now?

Except wring the story of Opal's death out of him?

Since Ariel was out of the office, Kline offered to help with any "secretary stuff" she had lying around. She accepted because it felt too awkward not to, but there wasn't much he could do without first learning the software they used to organize client files and keep appointments.

Trying to teach Kline to work a computer was only slightly less difficult than training a housecat to do a backflip through a Hula-Hoop.

"You click just here to open a new window." Winter reached over his shoulder and pointed at the screen. "You have to double-click."

"Double?" His face contorted into a mess of confusion. "Why double?"

"Why double?" Winter's heart sank all the way down into her shoes. "I don't know. You just do."

"Okay." He double-clicked but did it so slowly that the computer didn't register it. "Come on, you little bastard."

Winter pinched the bridge of her nose. At this rate, she was going to waste her entire day trying to teach Kline how to use a computer—a mouse!—and get absolutely no work done. Years of being an old-fashioned, railroading vagabond had left his technological skills planted firmly in the last millennium. If only she had a radio dial for him to tune or a pair of rabbit ears on a tube tv that needed jimmying.

The truth was, she could handle sorting through her own client files, or Noah could help out when he came in. There was no reason to push Kline this far out of his comfort zone.

Winter had a strong sense that he was enjoying himself about as much as she was. She wanted to tell him she was all right, thank him for everything, cut him a check, and send him on his merry way. But she didn't want to hurt his feelings. Besides, she was positive he only came into the office out of a sense of chivalry. Like Noah, he didn't feel comfortable with Winter being alone. He wanted to keep an eye on her, keep her safe.

She wasn't a freaking toddler, and she didn't need a babysitter.

Considering she was almost shot to death by crazed cosmetics entrepreneur Jessica Huberth and her lovesick henchman Kyle Fobb just about where they were standing, Winter was trying to be indulgent with the men in her life who worried for her safety. But her patience and her nerves were wearing thin. There was a strong whiff of patriarchal overprotection in the air, and it was starting to really irk her.

She watched him click again, trying to open the file, but so slowly that nothing happened. His finger on the mouse was a ten-pound weight.

Click...click...

Fire boiled inside, pressure building and threatening to erupt out of the top of her head. "That's enough. Thank you."

"Huh?" He looked up at her, his blue eyes just like hers, only wider and strangely innocent.

"Let's just forget about the computer and take a little break, okay? It's getting close to lunchtime."

It wasn't. The clock on the wall barely read eleven, and she usually ate closer to one, but it seemed a convenient excuse. This was an exercise in futility, and Winter couldn't take it anymore.

Kline didn't argue. In fact, he looked relieved. Rising from his chair, he followed her into the break room where she raided the fridge and threw together a couple of turkey and cheese sandwiches.

Without a word, Kline watched as she spread mayo and mustard on the bread. He sat at the circular table and drummed his fingers.

Smiling, she set his plate down in front of him and took a seat opposite.

He smiled back and took a bite.

They chewed in silence. The pressure was building again. All she wanted was to be alone in her own damn office.

But why? What was really going on inside her heart?

The opportunity for another father-daughter bonding session was at hand, but she didn't want to pressure him. Winter chewed her sandwich and tried for a fairly safe subject. "I'm glad you're feeling better."

Kline reddened. He'd seemed embarrassed to have tossed his cookies in front of her. He rubbed his stomach. "Yeah, thanks."

That's it?

She sighed. She might have to wring it from him after all. "Kline, we need to talk about—"

"It's about our family," he blurted, so loud she nearly jumped.

"What do you mean?"

"It's about you." He pointed at her. "You need to be careful. Whoever killed Opal is still out there, and they're coming here next."

She didn't understand. "Why do you think that?"

Kline shook his head. "You just have to trust me."

Naturally, that wasn't good enough. Winter didn't trust

her biological father. She had no reason to. Kline Hurst wasn't even his real name. Sure, he fessed up to being John Drewitt. But he'd shared the story about finding a homeless man dead in the road—and taking his ID—as an afterthought. Getting that much information out of him had been a minor miracle.

If that was even the whole story.

And Noah sure didn't trust him. He was still harping about turning the man in for identity theft. She was holding her husband at bay about that for now.

Without Kline's intervention, after all, she would have been fatally electrocuted. And he'd done good work for her since she brought him on at the office. She trusted he wasn't going to rob or murder her, and maybe that should've been enough.

But Winter took trust very seriously. She'd been badly burned too many times to ever give anyone, even family—*especially* family—the benefit of the doubt. And Kline was a hard person to trust, considering literally every move he's made since impregnating her mother was questionable.

Plus, Noah's trust instincts were usually spot-on.

She reached out a hand but let it drop an inch from his arm. "What happened to Opal?"

He choked, and she thought he'd throw up again. He swallowed several times but didn't run to the bathroom this time.

"I don't want to talk about it."

But you're the one who brought this up with me two days ago!

"I know it's hard." She kept her voice soft and free of judgment. "But you came to me and started the conversation."

He took a sip of water. "That was a mistake."

Irritation simmered under Winter's skin, and she bit it back. "You said I needed to brace myself, that I wouldn't like what you told me. If she'd passed from natural causes, I'd respect your wishes and never bring it up again. But she was murdered, and you seemed very convinced two seconds ago that the person who did it is coming after me next. Yet you won't tell me why."

"I was wrong."

The irritation bit back. "So you're just going to make me a sitting duck? Not tell me who or what to watch for. Some…"

Father you are.

She managed not to say it though.

Winter bit her bottom lip and looked down at the table. Anger pulsed in her brain like a boil about to pop. She took a deep breath to try to keep it down. "Please tell me."

He was silent for a minute—drinking water, staring, drinking. "You're not gonna like it."

"You keep saying that, but you won't know that for sure until you tell me."

His leg bobbed up and down, and he moaned as if in physical pain. "You're gonna think I'm crazy."

"Try me."

"Fine, but you have to promise you won't go to the police about this."

Anxiety tightened her chest "Why? Did you do something you shouldn't have?"

"The Philly police might not have anything on me, but that doesn't mean I'm completely in the clear. Until they catch who actually did this, I'm gonna be a suspect." Kline flexed his hand on the table. "And if they heard about…I mean, if you told them what I'm about to tell you, they'd think I was crazy. And that's not a good look on a murder suspect."

Winter sat up straighter. After two days of waiting, it was a long shot even bringing this up with Kline. She'd expected nothing more than another round of dodging and ducking this conversation. Now it seemed like there might actually be a legitimate reason, not just hunches and paranoia. Something real.

"Okay. I promise."

"And I know you're gonna tell Noah, so make sure he doesn't run his mouth off to the cops or Feds either."

She nodded. "Please. Will you just tell me?"

"All right." Kline took a deep breath and cracked all the knuckles in his fingers, one by one. "I was at Opal's house going through her things, trying to decide what was worth keeping. I went into her bathroom to answer the call of nature and noticed one of her business cards sitting on the sink. I knew it hadn't been there the last time I was in the bathroom an hour or so before that. Somebody had sneaked into the house and put it there while I was in her bedroom."

Winter pressed her hands between her knees. Her instinct was to start ripping holes in the story right away. "How can you be so sure the card wasn't there? Maybe you overlooked it?"

He wagged a finger at her. "There! That's why I didn't say nothin' the other day. I knew you'd think I was crazy."

She bit back a sharp retort. "I don't think you're crazy. I'm just trying to understand."

His nostrils flared, and he started peeling the label from the water bottle. "I knew the card hadn't been there before 'cause I'd washed my face. It was sitting on the edge of the sink. I would've seen it. And if I hadn't seen it, it would've been wet." He sighed in irritation. "Just trust me on this. I know I'm old, and you think I'm slow—"

She held up a hand. "You are not, and I do not."

A piece of the label came off in one long strip. "Just listen, okay? No questions 'til I'm done."

She pressed her lips closed. It was a tall order, but she'd try.

"The card had an address written on the back. It wasn't in Opal's handwriting. She was an old-fashioned, pretty cursive kind of a gal. This was block letters and all caps."

"Do you still have the card?"

"I said no questions." He mopped his forehead with his forearm. "I took the El from Frankford across town and ended up on two more trains and a couple of busses 'til I was in some neighborhood I'd never seen before. Real run-down area. I found the address, a tiny house with boarded-up windows, tagged with spray paint. Nobody lived there, but I noticed the lock on the old door was shiny and new. Somebody had even gone to the trouble of putting in a dead bolt."

Winter's interest was piqued. She sat forward and had to bite her lip to keep from interrupting.

"But when I tried the handle, it was unlocked. I walked inside, and…" He trailed off, his eyes darting. "A white banner was hung up in the front room, like for a party or something. And somebody had spray-painted on it the words, 'See you soon, Winter.'"

For a second, Winter's vision blurred around the edges. "Did you get a photo?"

Kline shook his head. "The camera on my phone's been broken for years."

"What else did you find?"

"I was freaked out, so I took out my pocketknife. I called out. Nobody answered. Then I walked through the house. Most of it looked like you'd expect. Empty, broken down. I found half a pizza in the refrigerator, but there wasn't any electricity going to it. There was a futon in the kitchen, too, that looked and smelled like someone had been sleeping there." Kline swallowed hard. "And in the bedroom, I found a cardboard canvas as big as the wall with a collage of photos and printouts and screenshots taped all over it."

"Photos of what?"

Kline closed his eyes, sucking a breath through his nostrils. "You."

Her chest tightened. "What kind of pictures?"

"Articles written about you. Printouts from your social media. Screenshots from surveillance videos. I didn't get a really good look at all of it though, 'cause as I was standing there, somebody came up from behind and put me in a choke hold. I tried to swing my knife on them, but they slammed me hard into the wall and knocked it out of my hand."

Winter's hand went to her mouth.

"They choked me out. When I woke up on the floor, they were gone. The banner was gone too. Even the pizza from the fridge. They took everything with them. The collage, everything."

Anger seared through her. "Why the hell didn't you tell me this before?"

"Because I didn't want you to think I was lying or crazy. I don't have any proof of anything, but I swear I saw it. They wanted me to see it. They're trying to scare you and get in your head. And mine."

"You should've called the cops yourself."

He shook his head. "They'd never believe me. Besides, the guy took all the evidence with him."

"They could've swept the place for prints, other evidence."

"Maybe, but I doubt it. I don't know if you've noticed, but people like me don't have the best relationship with law enforcement." Kline grimaced and picked at a callus on his palm. "More likely they'd just throw me in jail for a few days and interrogate me more about Opal."

Pushing back from the table, Winter launched to her feet. "Dammit. You should've told me."

Her brain pummeled her with memories of Carl Gardner—the stalker who'd installed surveillance cameras to spy on her. Who was deeply involved in the online fandom for her serial killer little brother. He'd been just one of many people who wanted to finish the work Justin started, no matter the cost.

Justin had planned to kill Winter.

"See you soon..."

"You think he's coming to Austin?"

And you waited two days to warn me?

"If he's not already here." Kline nodded solemnly. "I bought my Greyhound ticket that same night."

Winter pressed two fingers against her temple. A migraine was coming on. "Do you still have the business card?"

Kline fetched out a tiny, yellowed square from his wallet and passed it over.

On the front was a logo that looked like periwinkle on top of a wedding cake along with Opal's name and contact info. Winter had no idea her aunt had run a bakery. Learning that made her sad, the loss of the aunt she never knew hitting harder than it had yet.

She flipped the card over and narrowed her eyes at the address written on the back in black ink. She was no expert, but it looked like a man's handwriting to her. All caps like the person was shouting, *Go here. See this. I got it all ready for you.*

It was exactly as Kline said.

"See you soon, Winter."

7

I was very young when I learned that the best lies contained a grain of truth. My father taught me that. I supposed I was grateful. Although, if it weren't for him, I might never have needed to know such a thing.

People trusted their minds entirely too much when, in fact, the human brain was exceedingly malleable. Wired for survival, not truth.

Take the nose, for example. We could choose to look at our own noses, but normally we didn't. Our brains conveniently edited out our noses so they didn't interfere with the important things—like detecting saber-toothed tigers or appropriate mates.

Similarly, the human brain could edit something *in* that never actually happened. By starting with a little grain of truth—especially one wrapped in emotion—it was possible to create a memory more powerful than factual events that took place in a person's past.

Clarissa Toler, for example. She suffered a lonely, neglected childhood. Both her parents were career people, logical to the point of coldness, who constantly brushed off their daughter's needs and fears as meaningless childhood nonsense.

At the same time, they were overprotective, forbidding their daughter from spending time with friends. She longed for a companion, someone who could be there as her parents dragged her off on vacations that were more about the two of them as a couple than about the three of them as a family. She wanted a sibling—a brother or sister.

That was never going to happen. So little Clarissa, always a very imaginative girl, created one. In her therapy sessions, she spoke of a doll that she used to call Little Brother. It was an old Cabbage Patch Doll—the kind with yarn hair that collectors in the eighties went crazy for. She treated the toy with care and affection, creating adventures for him to go on, dressing him in little outfits, and sleeping with him clutched in her arms at night.

My fingers brushed over the notes in Clarissa's file laid open before me on my desk. A description of the day she lost that doll. That event had a deep, powerful effect on the little girl. It was one of those moments that constituted the inevitable loss of innocence all children underwent, provided they lived long enough.

Clarissa told me she'd been sitting alone on a lakeshore. Her parents were somewhere else, ignoring her as usual. She was playing with her doll when she got distracted by something—she couldn't even remember what anymore—and turned her back on Little Brother.

When she looked back, he was slowly bobbing away in the choppy water. She started to go after him, but the water was so cold—like needles stabbing into her skin. She drew back and watched the doll get swallowed by the dark ripples. She described her fear in that moment in such powerful detail—Clarissa was a talented wordsmith, after all—that she sounded like she'd lost a person, not a toy.

That was where I found my opportunity. I knew the plan could work, at least in theory, and Clarissa became subject one. She'd been undergoing EMDR, neurofeedback, and hypnosis at the office, so her brain was already open and malleable. She trusted in the process and in her practitioner, and that was all the foundation I needed.

It took several sessions to fully implant the memory. Bit by bit, I removed the word *doll* from her memory so that only *Little Brother* remained.

On our fourth go at it, Clarissa manifested the name *Clark* for this fictional dead boy. I didn't question it. I let her rich imagination fill in whatever details it wanted. Everything leading up to that day was her own domain. All I needed was for her to believe one simple line of thinking.

She had a little brother. She watched him die. And it was all her fault.

The plan worked almost perfectly. Though I thought Clarissa's strong imagination made her a perfect candidate, I was not so naive as to think a single personality trait predicted susceptibility to hypnotization. Most people could not be hypnotized at all, regardless of method. However, because of my previous clinical work, I knew Clarissa could be. Though to a lesser extent than someone like subject eleven, Perry Bick.

That man was as malleable as wet clay.

MRI evidence suggested the ability to be hypnotized was a matter of altered functional connectivity in the brain's networks. Not exactly something that could be deduced through standard analysis—and unfortunately, in most cases, that was all I had to go on.

I hadn't wanted to get my hands dirty, but there was a reason I stayed with Clarissa that night after the impromptu session at her apartment. She'd been confused when I showed up at her door, but a little hypnosis was enough to convince her to invite me in…and then to convince her I wasn't there at all. I became like a shadow lurking in the back of her brain, a phantom force gently pushing her toward the edge.

The power I possessed was intoxicating.

But I was disappointed with the final result. In the end, I figured, Clarissa suspected something was amiss with her implanted memory. She'd been on the very edge of suicide—literally—when something made her pull back, giving me no choice but to step in and finish the job.

Fortunately for me, Clarissa was petite. If she was larger, we'd have scuffled, and I wouldn't have had the strength to push her off. There was a reason I used my wits and not my muscles to accomplish my aims. Mother Nature had given me too much of one and not enough of the other. In this life, you had to work with what you had.

Looking down at the file lying open in front of me, I realized I'd scratched out Clarissa's face with my pen. My subconscious at work. One down and who knew how many more to go before I brought my real target down.

All in good time, I reminded myself.

My shoulders ached from the tussle with Clarissa. The arc of descent had to match the arc of a suicide. Though colloquially referred to as *jumpers*, people who threw themselves off buildings or bridges usually just leaned out and let go. And I'd pushed her. Hard. My muscles had been so tense through the whole thing, I was pretty sure I pulled every one of them.

I'd set something in motion the other night at Clarissa's, and now there was no going back.

Finally, after all these years, I would get my revenge. I was irritated, though, that the news coverage made no mention of foul play. The cops really seemed to think it was suicide.

I took the photo of Clarissa with her blacked-out face and

slipped it into my bag, a memento of the beginning of the end.

My phone rang in my pocket, startling me. I checked the number and groaned. My *partner*, as he liked to call himself. I had to be grateful to Erik, though. He was the catalyst that finally convinced me to create a plan and take action. A plan that, without him, would've remained a fuzzy fantasy in my brain. Still, there was something about him I didn't quite trust. And he was the bossiest "partner" on the planet.

When all this was over, our association would end, one way or the other. For now, I put up with him.

I answered. "Yes?"

"It's working."

"What is?"

"One of the subjects consulted with Winter Black. I saw him in her office. I knew this would all come together." Erik sounded calm and clear, which meant he was happy. When he got too excited, he stuttered and got repetitive.

I didn't give two shits about Winter Black. She was his obsession, his quarry. I couldn't even remember what she'd done to him. I didn't care. "Great. Which one?"

"Perry Bick."

"I don't think—"

But he didn't let me get farther than that. "Bick's your pick. I need Winter's attention."

"Fine." I scratched my eyebrow with the edge of my thumb. "But I don't want Winter Black poking her nose into my business." Bick would be a cinch. It was the detective I was worried about.

"This is my operation, my operation." His voice thundered through my phone, and I held it an inch away from my ear. "I scratched your back and got you into position. Now it's your turn, your turn to play ball. I'll be damned if you screw this up for me!"

He hung up, leaving me to roll my eyes. Winter, Winter, Winter. It was all he ever talked about. As sweet as it was to finally be taking my revenge after all these years, I'd be glad when all this was over, if only to be rid of Erik.

Although, for my revenge to cause the most suffering, I did need to pile up some bodies.

8

Just as Kline finished his story, a delivery driver arrived with a package for Winter. She opened it up, grateful for the distraction, and found the security cameras Noah had ordered. Kline quickly volunteered to install them. He wouldn't be able to handle the camera setup on the app, but he could certainly mount the gadgets.

After sending him off on his task, Winter entered her office and shut the door. It made her feel guilty, but she was glad to be rid of him. Everything about his story of finding the house was infuriating, particularly that it had taken him so long to fess up—not seventeen years long, but still.

Winter wasn't quite sure what to do with the information. She'd promised not to go to the police, but that promise meant less to her than catching a stalker who might be trying to kill her. One thing she knew for certain, she wanted to talk to Noah before making a definitive move in any direction. He already wanted her to tell the police about the *John Drewitt aka Kline Hurst* situation. She basically knew what he'd say about this.

She tried to call, but Noah's phone went straight to voicemail. He was probably still in his final debriefing.

Sitting around worrying about what Kline had seen was doing Winter absolutely no good, so she tried distracting herself with the case at hand—the case of Perry Bick, the blackmailer, and the fake flyers.

She texted Perry and asked if he could come to the office to answer a few more questions. Then she set down her phone and studied the flyer in its little plastic baggie.

Winter didn't believe in coincidences. Two of these fake flyers had been found so far, one accompanied by a blackmail letter and the other on the eve of the recipient's suicide. She wondered if she ought to call Lessner to let him know about the second letter. If Darnell had been in town, she certainly would've shared the information. But she didn't know the other detective.

If she told him about Perry and his blackmail case, Lessner might insert himself in the middle of it, which might spook her new client into silence. And then Winter would be up a certain creek, since he was her only lead.

All she knew for certain was that Clarissa Toler and Perry Bick both received a copy of the phony flyer. She tapped her finger against the edge of her desk. If Clarissa and Perry had something in common, if they knew each other, that was where she needed to start.

This was the part where she normally called out to Ariel and asked her to look into both of them—to comb through their places of work, their friends, their family, and especially their history and social media. Winter could then push that out of her mind and refocus on something else, knowing that within a few hours, Ariel would have some concrete answers.

But the desk sat empty. Winter sighed, wondering if her tech-savvy, Gen Z assistant would ever come back. After what had happened to her last week, she might've already decided this line of work was not her cup of coffee.

Winter's phone buzzed with a text. Perry wasn't available for the rest of the day, but he'd come by the office first thing tomorrow morning.

As she typed in her reply, the phone rang. Noah.

She breathed out a smile and answered. "At last."

"Well, it's official. I have no badge. I have no gun. I am completely naked."

"Put your clothes back on, silly boy. You're gonna get yourself arrested."

"It went well with Weston. Better than I expected."

"Who's Weston?"

"Falkner."

She laughed.

"Very funny. But you know, he's a good guy, actually. I don't hate him."

"Well, that is a glowing assessment if I ever heard one." She shook her head, relieved that Noah's final review had gone well.

Part of her wanted to blurt out everything she'd just learned from Kline, but she thought better of it. This was Noah's moment. And her stuff was the kind of news that needed to be delivered in person anyway. "What do you say we go out to dinner tonight to celebrate?"

"Celebrate?" He sounded confused. "Okay. I hadn't really thought of it that way."

"Well, I have." And once he was feeling a little tipsy and his belly was full of steak, he'd take the news of Kline's story much better. She hoped. "Where are you now?"

"Me and Eve are gonna grab some lunch, then I'll head to your office."

"Okay. See you soon."

"Love you." Winter kissed the air so Noah could hear it before she hung up.

A knock came at main door. Kline stood on the other side of the glass, a camera mount in his hands. She rose to answer and untwisted the lock. "Yes?"

"So this location and angle should give you the most coverage of the inside of the office, except in the bathroom. I was thinking we might want to put a few facing out, as well, both at the street and the back alley behind the building. That way, you'll be able to keep an eye on anybody approaching from any direction."

On first impression, Kline's suggestion seemed paranoid, but Winter reminded herself that it wasn't paranoia if people really were out to get her. And the idea of being able to watch someone approach her office long before they ever saw her appealed to her on a visceral level.

"Do it." Winter gave a decisive nod. Then she stepped around him and headed down the block.

What had happened to Ariel last week might've been a different story if they'd had cameras. And the new setup could go a long way toward getting Winter's assistant back in the office.

9

Noah pulled up to Winter's office and parallel parked his massive truck between two tiny cars. As he stepped out, he spotted Kline on a small ladder out front with a drill in his hand. Noah tossed his keys in the air, caught them, and shoved them into his pocket, approaching the door with a bounce in his step. He was feeling oddly good—lighter and easier. Breezy, even.

He smiled at Kline as he stepped toward the door. "Afternoon."

Kline startled, wobbling on the ladder. "Oh, hello. What are you doing here?"

"I'm officially on sabbatical."

"That's a relief." Kline finished screwing in a bolt and climbed down from his stepladder. "Hey, could I talk to you for a second?"

"Uh, yeah." Noah peeked through the glass. "Where's Winter?"

"She headed toward that coffee place she likes." He wiped some dirt from his hand onto his pants and slid a screwdriver into his tool belt. "I was getting these mounted, but you'll have to get the setup rocking and rolling. I don't think I want to touch another computer again as long as I live."

Noah smirked. "Good luck with that."

"Look…" he scratched his ear, "this isn't working for me. I think I need to cut out."

"No problem. I'm on it. Where'd you leave the box with the manual?"

"No, you don't get it." He hunched his shoulders in a gesture of misery and guilt. "I mean cut out of the city. For good. The box is in the break room, on the counter."

Noah paused, rolling the words back and forth through his mind. "You're leaving again." He found himself awash with anger when he should've been feeling relief. The man blew into town and found a way to cling to Winter when she didn't even know he was her father, and now that she did know, he wanted to leave? There was something ass-backward about that, even considering he didn't trust the man.

"I've done all I can do here." Kline set his hands on his hips and looked vaguely into the distance. "But this whole situation isn't working. Not for me and not for Winter. She's too nice to say anything, but I can tell I'm driving her crazy."

"No, that's not it. It's just awkward, you know? She lost most of her family so long ago. I don't think she ever expected—"

"Don't try to change my mind." Kline focused his gaze back on Noah. "I know what I am, and I know what I'm not. Right now, I'm just a millstone around her neck. Christ knows she already has enough of those. And I gotta be honest, I'm a rolling stone. Here in Austin, I'm growing moss all over me. I think I'm headed out to Nevada. I got a friend there who needs help fixing his attic. He'll put me up in his RV for a while, and then…I'll go wherever the wind takes me."

Noah studied the man. Did he want Kline gone? He contemplated that for a moment before realizing it didn't matter. Dampening his own emotions with a metaphorical watering hose, he focused instead on what would be best for his wife.

He wasn't sure Winter wanted Kline gone for good, and Noah didn't want Kline's actions to hurt Winter, either now or in the long run. Noah wanted her biological father to take responsibility for his past actions and make up for past harm.

"You don't have to skip out, Kline. We've got plenty of work for you here. If you're all done at the office, I got a bunch of land that needs tilling before I can plant my garden."

Kline ran his hand over his thinning gray hair. "I appreciate everything you two have done for me. I really do. And there's a part of me that wishes I could go back in time and give Jeannette a chance to tell me when she got pregnant. Maybe I would've stuck around and there never would've been any space for Bill Black or Kilroy or Justin to come into her life. Winter could've grown up normal."

Noah frowned, the muscles tightening in his face. Thinking about all the horrible things Winter endured before he knew her was obviously painful, but more than that—it made him feel useless and impotent, as illogical as that was. "If you'd known, would you have stayed and done the right thing?"

"I would've tried. The question is, would Jeannette have had me? We both knew she was out of my league."

"Have you talked to Winter about leaving yet?"

Kline shook his head. "I'm not sure how to bring it up."

"I think she'll argue with you." Noah knew she would. And if she did convince the man to stay, it would be after a trip to the precinct and a confession about identity fraud. It might've been a big ask, but that was what Noah would need if Kline was going to stick around.

"I thought of that." Kline fiddled with the hammer hanging from his tool belt, spinning it in its holder. "Someone's after her. The person who killed my sister."

"What?"

"I'm not gonna get into it right now, but Winter believes me." He wouldn't meet Noah's eyes. "The fact is, if this guy's willing to kill my sister to try to get to Winter, then he'll happily kill me too. I'm one-hundred-percent certain the reason I'm still alive right now is he wanted me to bring this 'story' back to tell Winter. Now that I've done that…the next time he catches me alone, it's gonna be curtains. And Winter doesn't need another dead relative weighing on her."

Noah gritted his teeth. "So you're scared, basically?"

"Hell yes, I'm scared!" Kline coughed out an incredulous laugh. "Anybody with half a brain would be scared. Besides, you're on sabbatical now, right? So you'll be here to protect her and keep her safe?"

"Of course I will."

"And you'll do a better job of it than I ever could. She's lucky to have you."

"I'm the lucky one."

Kline sighed, then clapped his hand lightly on Noah's shoulder. "I know my approval doesn't mean much, but you're a good son-in-law."

Noah looked at his hand and back at his face. He was right. It didn't mean much. "Are you just gonna take off again without a word, or are you actually gonna talk to Winter?"

"I'll talk to her first. I promise." He glanced through the glass into the office, his eyes squinting against the sunlight. "I know it doesn't seem like much. It *isn't* much. But these little projects I've done are really all I can do for her. And the place is in pretty good shape now."

That was true. "It is."

Turning from the window, Kline tilted his head up to look right into Noah's eyes. "I've done what I can to try to hide the truth from her, but I'm not a good person. I'm barely a person at all."

From the start, Noah had struggled to decide if Kline was trustworthy. Something about that admission finally clinched it for him. Kline could be trusted regarding his loyalty to Winter. And Noah didn't think he was a bad person. But he was a loner with secrets Noah could never pry loose.

"When do you plan to leave?"

"Soon."

"Good luck out there." Noah shook his hand. "Will we be hearing from you again?"

"I don't want to lie, so best not to say either way." Kline released his hand and went back to fiddling with his hammer. "I swear I'll talk to Winter before I go. Just keep this under your hat until I do, okay?"

A grinding sound emanated from Noah's throat. "Me and Winter don't keep secrets from each other."

"Not a secret. Just a delayed truth."

The sound continued. "I'll give you twenty-four hours, but that's it. I can't bend any more than that."

"Thank you." Kline smiled, lopsided so only one tiny dimple showed. "And thank you for loving my daughter the way she deserves to be loved. There aren't nearly enough guys like you out there in the world."

The compliments made Noah uncomfortable. He had a strange urge to hug his impromptu father-in-law but quashed it like so many pointless impulses.

He stepped up to the door and swung it open. The bounce was gone from his step, familiar melancholy sweeping back in. Winter was going to be upset in more ways than one. But perhaps, for just one night, they'd be able to sweep everything under the rug and actually find a way to have some fun together.

10

After Noah finished connecting all the security cameras to the app, he decided to walk to a nearby park. The sun was warm, and the most recent spring rains had made their way through, leaving nothing but clear skies to enjoy. Kline was hanging out in the office waiting for Winter, presumably to tell her the truth about his plans to leave and likely never come back.

Noah had more questions for his father-in-law. Was he going to cut off contact with his daughter completely? How long did he plan to stay in Nevada? Would he ever return? But the more he thought about it, the more Noah realized he didn't really want answers. He didn't trust Kline as far as he could throw him, so nothing the old man said could assuage his doubts.

Better to just get out of the way and mind his own business. Besides, he'd given Kline a full twenty-four hours to break the news to Winter. That meant Noah had a full twenty-four hours during which he had to keep a secret. From his wife. One of the best investigators in the United States.

The less time he spent around Winter, the easier that would be.

He settled onto a stone park bench, closed his eyes, and inhaled the aroma of mint and pine. He exhaled and did it again. Noah told himself to be present and let go of some of his issues for just a few quiet minutes. It wasn't often he got to relax on benches in the middle of a workday.

Across the field, a young boy approached a swing set. The kid looked around and spun in a full circle before deciding against swinging and opting to go sit on a similar bench.

Noah looked around. There wasn't an adult anywhere nearby. The kid didn't look any older than six or seven, so that didn't make much sense. Maybe his mom was in the bathroom or something.

In his hands, Noah turned over a little white half sphere of plastic and glass—a Wi-Fi camera Kline had found attached to the roof of Black Investigations while installing the new security system. It was the same make as the other cameras Carl Gardner had put there.

Based on the weathered look of it, the camera had likely been there for at least a few weeks, and Noah had simply missed it when he was cleaning up the others. He wondered if it had still been broadcasting all this time, filming Winter, Ariel, Kline, and himself as they moved in and out of the office.

Carl Gardner was dead, but that didn't mean they weren't still being watched. Gardner hadn't worked alone.

When Noah looked into his background, Gardner's social media history revealed a general hatred of women and a fascination with the men who made it their business to kill them. Gardner had found his way to Justin Black's fan site, where he was indoctrinated into the club and exploited for his technical skills.

The specifics of Gardner's involvement wouldn't be

confirmed until the report from computer forensics came back. As it stood, Noah had no idea how many people might be involved in stalking Winter or who they were. Right now, all he had to go on were his own educated guesses.

Whoever Carl was working for, Noah seriously doubted they would give up so easily. So the question remained, what would they do next?

Now that he was on sabbatical, Noah had the time to find the answer to that question. The freedom to give Winter all the backup and support she needed. To smoke out all the people who were involved in this sick conspiracy against his wife. He'd give her back her privacy and her security if it was the last thing he ever did.

And then…what?

Weston Falkner's words kept going around in his head like a song. *"This next year will be a good time to have all those conversations, with yourself at the very least. And don't wait too long. Have your children young enough that you'll be alive to play with your grandchildren."*

Again, Noah glanced across the field at the little boy on the bench. He wondered why he hadn't chosen to play on the swing set.

But then his mind started to wander. He imagined pushing his own kids on those swings, empty but swaying in the breeze. He heard the phantom trill of laughter in the back of his brain, a little girl with blue eyes and black hair squealing as she begged her daddy to push her higher and higher.

Noah blinked, fighting to keep himself from going too deeply into the fantasy. This was a nice park and so close to Winter's work. It'd be a great place to bring their kids.

Once again, he focused on the little boy. His sandy-brown hair was cut close to the scalp, his knees covered in brown scabs. His fingers gripped the edge of the bench tightly, and his head swung slowly from side to side, a touch of panic in his wide eyes.

Where're his parents? Is he really all alone?

Slipping the small Wi-Fi camera into his pocket, Noah rose to his feet and crossed the field, approaching the boy gingerly so as not to spook him.

Though he was a grown adult man, Noah was wary of children, especially little boys. The big, nasty scar left over when nine-year-old Tim Stewart stabbed his guts with a kitchen knife pulsed and ached. Before that happened, Noah had implicitly trusted children. Maybe not to tell the truth, but to not cause him severe physical harm.

He'd never make that mistake again.

"You doing okay, buddy?" Noah asked from about fifteen feet away.

The boy startled, his wide eyes latching onto Noah. He nodded, but his expression was a mask of panic and bottled-up fear.

On instinct, Noah reached for the badge he always kept in his pocket, knowing his credentials would help convince the boy to trust him.

But his badge wasn't there anymore.

That was going to take some getting used to.

The boy wiped his nose and shook his head. The skin under his eyes was red and bumpy with flush, as if he'd been crying.

"Where's your mom?" Noah asked.

The kid shrugged and looked out across the park. "I don't know. She was yelling at me, so I ran away. Now I don't know where she is or where I am." A tear sprang from his eye and journeyed down his cheek.

Noah took a cautious step closer. "Don't worry, buddy. We'll find her. When did you last see her?"

"We were in a store. I broke a glass squirrel, and she

yelled at me, so I ran away. I thought she would chase me, but...I don't know where I am now. I don't know where she is. I'm so stupid."

"Calm down." Noah crouched and took out his phone. "The store you were in, is it near here?"

The boy nodded.

"Do you remember what it was called?" Noah could think of a few places nearby that might sell decorative glass squirrels. There was a garden store stuffed with wind chimes, sundials, and charms maybe half a block to the west, as well as a very fancy pet shop just on the other side of the block. It wasn't a very long list.

"I don't know." Another tear fell down his cheek.

"That's okay. We'll figure this out. I bet your mommy is really worried about you."

The boy nodded and wiped his nose on his sleeve.

"What's your name?"

"Caleb."

"All right, Caleb. I'm Noah. It's nice to meet you." He showed Caleb his phone. "I'm gonna call the police, and they're gonna help us get you back to your mom, okay?"

He unlocked the screen and was scrolling through to find the nonemergency police number when he noticed another man walking toward them. He was about Noah's height, with dark hair and eyes and an impressively thick beard. He was dressed in a sharp navy blue tailored suit.

"Caleb?" The man jogged closer on thick black boots. "Is that you?"

Noah lowered his phone. "Do you know that man, Caleb?"

Caleb hesitated, then shook his head.

When the man reached them, he brushed right past Noah and knelt in front of where the boy was sitting. "Caleb?"

"Yeah?"

"Your mommy is very worried about you." The man took his phone from his pocket and tapped out a text. "I just told her where you are. She'll be here to pick you up soon."

Caleb nodded and pulled his legs up onto the bench, hugging his scabby knees tight to his chest.

"Thanks for keeping an eye on him." The man rose to his feet, dusting off his knees.

"No problem. You know his mom?" Noah studied his face, taking note of his angular features and age—maybe thirty on the high end.

He shook his head. "I was grabbing a quick lunch and ran into her on the street. Poor woman looked like she was about to lose her mind, so I offered to help."

"I can imagine." Noah put out his hand for a shake. "I'm Noah, by the way."

"Erik." He clasped his fingers, firm and cold as shark's skin. Probably an investment banker, although the beard was an unusual choice. "Yeah, I was just on my way to work when I saw her."

"It's kind of you to help." Noah pulled his fingers away from the man's lingering grip. "What do you do?"

Erik smiled. "A bit of this and that."

"This and that" in a tailor-made suit. Interesting.

A bright-red Toyota careened into the parking lot and squealed to a stop. With the engine still running, the door flew open, and a woman with long blond hair jumped out. Her head bobbed from side to side as she looked at each of them.

"Caleb!" She ran down the hill.

Caleb didn't gasp. He didn't grin. He didn't call back. He just jumped to his feet without a word and ran for her.

Standing shoulder to shoulder with Erik, Noah watched as mother and son raced toward each other and slammed into a hug in the middle of the field. Caleb's mother squeezed him and scolded him in roughly equal measure—a hug, a finger wag, a kiss on the head, a grimace. Caleb just kept trying to nuzzle into her and hide his face in her shoulder. He whispered to her, and she whispered back.

Slowly, Noah and Erik started toward them. As they approached, he noted the tears on her cheeks and the worry lines across her face. A frightened—and now very relieved—mother. Noah had seen so many of them in his years on the job.

Her gaze flicked to Erik, a glimmer of recognition at its core and a flat expression on her face.

"Thank you!" She clutched her son to her hip as she stood. "Thank you so much for finding him."

"No problem." Erik ruffled the boy's hair. "Glad to help."

"I better get him home now. We have a lot to talk about."

The mother gave another wave as she tightened her son to her side and led him back to the car. Caleb glanced over his shoulder, and Noah felt his eyes like hot beams of light slamming into his chest. The boy wasn't crying. His cheeks weren't red.

As he turned away, he whispered to his mom again. She just patted his head and kept walking.

There was something uncanny about the incident, something strange. Noah couldn't put his finger on it. More than likely, it was just his own suspicion and general discomfort projecting into the world.

"I guess our work here is done, huh?" Erik took earbuds from his pocket and shoved one in place.

Noah nodded. For a moment, he'd forgotten Erik was there. "It's always good to see a story like that have a happy ending."

He'd been up close and personal with far too many that didn't.

As the car pulled out of the lot, Erik gave Noah a lazy

salute, put in his other earbud, and meandered away, leaving Noah standing alone in the field and feeling vaguely uneasy. Whatever else he ended up doing while he was off work, he knew he wanted to keep helping people like Caleb find their way out of trouble and back to their happy endings.

Still, something was off. Like when a tiny prickly seed got caught in a shoe—too small to see, yet demanding attention with each step.

With a roll of his tight shoulders, Noah headed out of the park. That was enough relaxing for one day.

11

After picking up her latte, Winter took a long mental health stroll around the neighborhood.

No doubt she was distracted. As she walked around downtown, everything she and Kline had discussed cycled around and around in her head like a catchy tune. His story of what had happened in Philadelphia was so absurd, she wanted to dismiss it. Unfortunately, it wasn't exactly news that somebody was after her. She just wasn't sure who, or why, or how far they'd go to get whatever they wanted.

She wondered if the person who'd written the words *See you soon, Winter* wanted to take from her the same thing they had taken from Opal. Her life.

Of course, that was conjecture. She didn't know for certain the person who killed Opal was the same person who lured Kline to that abandoned house with some old pizza and a Winter shrine. It was damn good conjecture, but conjecture nonetheless.

She wasn't sure what her next move should be, other than speaking to Noah. He was going to be very upset, and rightly so. Her ex-marine, alpha-dog husband would probably go into full protector mode. Several times in the past, Noah had annoyed Winter by presuming to position himself as her sentinel.

This was not one of those times. In fact, the only thing in the world that would make her feel even remotely better about this was knowing Noah was on his guard, on her side, and doing everything he could to find the threat against her and destroy it.

By the time she got back to Black Investigations, her cardboard cup was empty and so was the office.

And the door had been left unlocked.

With an irritated sigh, Winter flicked on all the overhead lights as she entered and locked the door behind her. Before settling in her office chair, she yanked up every blind in her little fishbowl, giving her an unobstructed view of her surroundings. The bogus flyer and blackmail letter Perry Bick had brought to their consultation sat on her desk in their individual plastic baggies. Next to that was a paper with a handwritten exchange between Kline and Noah.

Kline wrote that Noah would finish setting up the cameras, and that he'd be back later. And in Noah's writing was a username and password, indicating he'd likely finished setting the cameras up.

She was staring at the notes when the front door jolted open, the sound pulsing through her blood like a shock. Winter jumped to her feet, hand going to her hip where her gun used to be.

When's that gonna stop?

She'd locked the door. She was certain of it.

Then she looked up to see Noah, keys in hand, and all at once, the tension left her like water draining from a bathtub.

"Hey, jumpy." Noah smiled. He held a brown paper bag that looked and smelled like food. Without looking back, he turned the latch and locked the door behind him. "I was hoping you'd be back. Where'd you go for coffee anyway? Milan?"

She walked across the room and threw her arms around Noah's neck. Feeling the solidness of his strong body, she let herself rest against him, the muscles in her back relaxing. Then she pecked him on the cheek and nuzzled into his neck. "I thought you'd be here when I got back."

"Kline was here, and I didn't want to—"

"Kline isn't here now."

Noah looked sour, though he was clearly trying to hide it. He kissed the top of her head and rested his cheek against it. "I got salads from Café Anaheim."

"Extra guac?"

"You know it, darlin'."

"Perfection." She pecked his lips, snatched the bag, and started toward the break room to find utensils.

"I went over to the park for a bit to decompress, but drama found me there too."

"What do you mean?" She set the bag down on the table and pulled out the aluminum bowls overfilled with lettuce, *pico de gallo*, and cotija cheese. The sandwich she'd made herself earlier still sat on the plate with only two bites taken out of it. After Kline had told her his terrible story, she'd lost her appetite. Now that Noah was here, her stomach was grumbling.

"Nothin' much." He pulled out a chair and took a seat, popping the seal on the plastic lid. "Little kid got mad at his mom, ran away, and got lost. We found the mom, though. It was good to see them reunited so quickly without much drama."

"Aw, that's nice." Winter opened the tomatillo dressing and drenched her salad. The smell of the Hatch chili beef across the top made her stomach gurgle even louder. It was not happy with her for abandoning lunch earlier. "Who's 'we?'"

"Just some Good Samaritan who was helping out. That was nice to see, too, you know? It's easy to forget sometimes in our line of work that most folks are basically good and want to help."

Winter nodded, trying to think back to the last time she'd had the pleasure of running into such a person. But her thoughts kept circling back to Kline and Opal and threatening notes spray-painted on banners.

"Everything all right?" Noah set his hand lightly on hers. Warm and gentle and as welcome as spring.

She squeezed his fingers and nodded. "I wonder if Kline'll be upset about you coming on board."

"What do you mean?"

"I think with Ariel being out for a while, he was hoping he could pitch in. I tried to train him on the computer this morning and…let's just say it didn't exactly go well."

"I wouldn't worry about that too much."

"What do you mean?"

He poked around at his salad, gathering beef and cheese and tortilla strips on his fork but not taking a bite. "I had a chat with him this morning. He seemed relieved I was going to be here working with you. I think he's actually pretty self-aware when it comes to his strengths and weaknesses, more than most people."

"Do you think he'll think I think he's not good enough?"

Noah dipped his head from side to side and made a little groaning sound in his throat. "He might think that, but only because it's true."

Winter smacked his shoulder. "Don't be such a shit."

"I'm just saying, he doesn't want to disappoint you. And he definitely doesn't want you feeling obligated to employ him if his help isn't actually helping. He's an observant guy.

He's not stupid. And I promise you, his feelings are not hurt."

Winter sat back and wrinkled her nose at her husband. "Sounds like you two have been talking about me."

"Well, yeah. What else do you expect us to talk about?"

"I don't know. Guy stuff. Football, maybe."

"It's offseason, honey."

Winter smiled softly as she watched his green eyes. She licked her lips and opened her mouth, ready to launch into all the bad news about Opal, when Noah beat her to it.

"So what are we working on these days? What's the case?"

Winter blinked, happy she had Perry and the flyers to discuss with Noah.

"I need you to look into my new client's background. Perry Bick."

"Why? Do you not believe his story?"

Winter weighed the question for a moment. "I do, but I don't. I think he thinks he's telling me the truth, but I'm just not sure."

"Why's that?"

Winter rose from her seat and went to her office to fetch the flyer and the blackmail letter. When she set them down in front of Noah, she summarized the drama surrounding the fake flyers. Clarissa Toler's suicide, Perry Bick's story about the strip club he worked at in Kentucky, and the guy who harassed him until he beat him into a coma.

Noah picked up the flyer, scanning it up and down. "Feels like a setup."

Winter waved her fork in the air before stabbing into her salad. "A rather circuitous one."

"So what else is new?"

"I don't know. I don't know if I can trust Perry. I don't even know if he really is being blackmailed."

"You said you think he's telling the truth."

"Yeah, I do." She swallowed a bit of chili. "But I don't think that's what happened. He doesn't even know the name of the man he beat into a coma seventeen years ago. Yet he seems to think he's still alive…somewhere…in this coma."

"Do you think he might've made the flyers?"

Winter sat beside Noah and scowled at the ugly, spartan design. "It's possible. Whoever made them is definitely screwing with me. I just don't know why or what their endgame might be. And both Perry Bick and Clarissa Toler, the children's author who died by suicide Friday evening, had these flyers. Why?"

"Whoever it is, it seems like they're trying to control which clients get sent your way. Everybody who's gotten one of these flyers on their door likely has something in common. If we can find that, then we can find who made them and why." Noah sipped his soda.

"Well, there's your first assignment, then. Dig into Perry Bick and Clarissa Toler. See if there's a connection. And see if you can find anything about this mystery man who's lived half his life in a coma somewhere in Madison County, Kentucky. Would be close to EKU, where the assault allegedly occurred."

"You got it, Boss." Noah waggled his eyebrows. "Anything else you need from me? You're looking pretty tense. Why don't you let me rub your back?"

Winter pursed her lips to hide a smile. "I don't think my husband would like that very much."

Noah's hand landed on her knee, slowly snaking toward her inner thigh. "What he don't know won't hurt him."

She'd scooched closer when a loud banging on the front door startled them both. Winter jumped up and raced out of the break room, Noah just behind her.

A large man with a bald head in a red button-down stood just beyond the door. After shaking the handle, he balled his hand into a fist and pounded on the door so hard, the whole office shook.

"Hey!" he cried when he caught sight of her and Noah. "You open or what?"

Noah stepped in front of Winter, his hand resting lightly on the .45 holstered at his hip. "Who are you? What do you want?"

"What's the big idea, asshole? You got something you want to say to me? Come out here and say it to my face!" He slammed his fist into the glass again, over and over.

"What the hell are you talking about?" Noah shouted back. "You need to calm down before I call the police."

"Go ahead! I'd love to hear you try to explain this!" The man slapped a piece of paper up against the window.

Winter leaned in closer to read it. Her heart leaped into her throat and then dropped like a lead weight. In the man's heavy, sweaty hand was yet another fake flyer.

12

"Open the damn door!" The man knocked so hard, the glass shivered.

Noah stomped closer, positioning himself in front of Winter like a protective dog. "You calm your ass down."

"Are you Winter Black?" The man glared past Noah. "How can you live with yourself, huh? This is how you drum up business for your so-called agency? You should be ashamed."

Yeesh, Perry Bick thought the flyer fell from the heavens, a sign from the universe to reach out for help.

Winter stepped up to stand shoulder to shoulder with Noah. "I have no idea what you're talking about."

"Yeah, right." The laughter that burst from his thick throat was cruel and hollow. A vein on his bald head bulged and pulsed pale green against his warm brown skin. His eyes were large and froglike. He was at least as tall as Noah, with the musculature to match any marine, but the way he was dressed suggested a desk job of some sort.

"I'm here to give you your disgusting blackmail letter.

The joke's on you. I'd rather the whole world know my dirty little secret than pay you one red dime."

"I didn't send the letter or the flyer." Winter brushed past Noah before he could stop her and opened the lock.

"Winter…" Noah warned, drawing closer.

"It's fine." She pulled open the door, standing face-to-face with the fuming man. "Please, calm down so we can discuss this like rational adults."

He stepped over the threshold and crossed his arms, the papers in his hand wrinkling against his chest. "I'm calm as a damn cucumber, honey."

"Good." She crossed her arms too. "Now what's your name?"

"You know damn well what my name is."

"Let's assume I don't."

"Robin Sheen, aka the poor son of a bitch you're trying to squeeze every last drop out of." He threw the flyer and another paper at her feet like a gauntlet he expected her to pick up.

After eyeing it for a moment, Winter glanced back at Noah. "Will you grab a glove and some evidence bags out of my desk? That's Noah, by the way. And you know my name."

Noah didn't move right away, his gaze shifting between Robin Sheen, the papers, and Winter. Once he seemed convinced this guy wasn't about to launch himself at his wife like an attack dog, Noah turned and headed for her office.

"Now, please, start at the beginning. Where did you find these?"

"Where did I find them?" Robin jabbed his forefinger at Winter. "I found them exactly where you left them."

Fighting the urge to swat his finger away from her face, Winter planted her hands on her hips. "And where was that?"

"Under the windshield wiper of my truck out in a gas

station parking lot. It's a pretty stupid scheme, if you ask me. Terrify people with exposure unless they pay for your services."

"That would be a pretty stupid scheme. Why would I want to blackmail you *and* have you as a client? Doesn't it seem idiotic to give you my name, phone number, and business location when all you need to send me money is an email address?"

"Yeah. It's really stupid."

Winter stepped back when Noah returned. With a gloved hand, he scooped up the papers and placed them into individual plastic bags.

"That's because it's not true." She took the notes from Noah and held them up. "These flyers did not come from my office. Whoever's trying to blackmail you is also screwing with my business and my reputation. We're both victims of the same letter writer. And you're the third person to receive one of these fake flyers. I'm still trying to figure out who's doing it and why."

She scanned the flyer. It was—with the exception of Robin's name at the top—identical to the others. The blackmailer was even asking for the same amount of money.

"Do you know what secret the blackmailer is referring to?"

Robin's lips twitched. "Yes. I only have one secret worth blackmailing me over, but it sure as hell isn't worth thirty grand. I made up my mind last night that I'd just start spreading the news my damn self. Take the ammunition out of this asshole's hands. As a matter of fact, getting this letter spurred me on to finally make things right after all this time."

Winter tilted her head. "Would you mind telling me?"

He hesitated a moment, his pale-brown eyes watching her as if he was trying to make up his mind about something. At last, he shrugged. "Might as well."

"Come. Have a seat." Winter gestured toward the sitting area near the back of the open office, beyond the receptionist desk where Ariel used to sit. Where Noah would be sitting until further notice.

With tight fists and even tighter shoulders, Robin skulked inside and sat down. "When I was in college, I cheated on my girlfriend. With her mother."

Winter took a seat across from him, fighting not to let her disgust appear on her features. Naturally, she'd seen, heard, and experienced far worse than this as an investigator, but she rarely met a person who disclosed such information without beating around the proverbial bush.

Noah stood just beyond her right shoulder, ready to pounce at a moment's notice.

Winter grabbed her notepad. "Go on."

"Ain't nothing to go on about. The mother got pregnant, and we decided…I mean, I convinced her…she needed an abortion." Robin folded his arms across his chest. "She agreed and went to the clinic the next day. We broke it off right after that. Me and the mother, and me and my girlfriend. I never told her the truth. Not until yesterday."

"This is your ex from college, you said, which would've been over a decade ago, correct?"

"Doesn't mean it was okay, just because it didn't happen last week." Robin was getting worked up all over again.

"I'm just thinking about the timeline." Winter motioned for him to continue.

Robin laughed dryly, shaking his head. "So anyway, I called up my ex and confessed the truth. I told her that I didn't expect her to forgive me, but I needed her to know I was sorry." Any hint of laughter in his voice died away. "The thing is, she tried to argue with me about it."

"Argue with you about your apology?"

He kept shaking his head, over and over. It was beginning

to make Winter dizzy. "It's ridiculous. I don't even know what to do with it."

"Take it one step at a time." Winter took a deep breath through her nose. Well, her one nostril that wasn't blocked, hoping Robin would unconsciously mirror the calming gesture.

He did. People almost always did.

"What did your ex-girlfriend say when you confessed to her?"

"She told me to stop making up stupid, terrible lies."

"She didn't believe you?"

"According to her, when we were dating, her mom was living on the other side of the country. She said I never even met her mother."

Winter glanced at Noah. He looked as confused as she felt. Robin Sheen's story was beginning to hold about as much water as Perry Bick's. The man in the coma was not only nameless but couldn't be tracked down, and Robin had never even met his girlfriend's mother.

Playing devil's advocate, Winter asked, "You mean the woman you had sex with lied to you about being your girlfriend's mother?"

"No. That's not possible. Jessie's the one who introduced me to her. We all had dinner together. I remember what I ordered, and what we—"

"Okay." She rubbed the back of her neck and rolled her head slightly from side to side to dispel the sudden ache there. "Did you speak to the mother? Call her to verify?"

"Yeah. I asked for her phone number. Jessie was real confused and didn't want to give it to me. Instead, she got us all on a three-way…" He shook his head again and tossed his arms up in the air. "No pun intended."

Winter side-eyed Noah. "Okay, so Jessie's mother came on the line. And?"

"I didn't recognize her voice. I mean, at all. And she said the same thing Jessie did. That we never met. In the end, they both got really frustrated with me and hung up, telling me to get my head checked and never bother them again."

"Is it possible you're confusing one girlfriend for another?"

"Don't you think I thought of that? So yeah, I called the only other girlfriend I had in college, but she was raised by her grandpa. She doesn't even have a mom." Robin rested his elbows on his knees and dropped his head into his hands. "I think I'm going crazy. And I'm already in therapy, by the way, so that ain't gonna help."

Winter wouldn't argue that going crazy was one potential explanation. If she had not met Perry Bick and were she not looking at her third fake flyer and second blackmail note, she would've put that theory near the top of her list. But two thirtysomething men, who appeared to be sober and coherent, had come into her office within hours of each other to confess to horrible past wrongdoings that Winter was not convinced ever happened.

She pressed her palms flat on her desk. "I could see the mother being motivated to lie about an affair with her daughter's boyfriend, but I don't know why they would try to convince you that you'd never even met her."

"No. It's more than that." Robin clenched his eyes shut and wiped his sweaty palms on his pants. The anger seemed to have drained out of him, leaving behind a vague kind of fear—pale and quiet. "I went on social media and looked up Jessie's account. I found pictures of her mother and…" He smacked himself in the forehead. "It's not her."

"The mother?"

"Jessie's mom…the woman I got pregnant, was a sexy redhead. A voluptuous Jessica Rabbit type. Her actual mom, and I looked at pictures from back then too, was…"

"And what?"

His face reddened. "I don't know how to say this without sounding like an asshole, but she looks like a potato."

Winter massaged her temple with her finger and thumb. "So who did you get pregnant?"

"I don't know. No one, I think."

"What do you mean?"

"Look, I've been thinking about this horrible incident from my past nonstop for the last couple of weeks, but I don't remember ever thinking about it before then. And the guilt I've been carrying around feels fresh, too, if that makes sense. I know it sounds insane. Impossible."

"You're right, it does. But that doesn't mean you're wrong." Winter met her husband's eyes again, his expression cautious and curious. "So Robin. Let's pretend that this whole story didn't actually happen, at least not the way that you remember it. How could anyone know about it, you know, to blackmail you with it?"

His lips parted, but then he sealed them back up and didn't answer.

Winter sucked in a deep breath. "One thing I can tell you is you aren't the only person the so-called Listener has been targeting."

"Really?" Hope burst to life in his expression and voice. "Who else?"

"One target is a client, so I can't reveal any information about them. But clearly, the other target is me. So far, the blackmailer has sent out two letters alongside fake flyers for my business. Whoever the Listener is, they have it in for both of us."

And Perry Bick. And they've very likely already gotten to Clarissa Toler.

Now that she'd encountered Robin Sheen and his strange story, Clarissa's death seemed even less likely to be a suicide.

For the first time, Robin looked at her with something other than disdain in his eyes. "But if it's all in my head…if it didn't even happen…what the hell does that mean?"

Winter chewed on her knuckle. If she could find a connection between Robin, Perry, and Clarissa, she would get much closer to identifying the blackmailer and discovering what they really wanted, other than money.

Was the real goal to convince these people to take their own lives?

If Robin was being blackmailed over something that never actually happened, it was possible Perry was too. Even though he had the date and location of the crime, according to the Kentucky authorities, no man had been beaten into a coma seventeen years ago. Did that mean Robin did not have an affair with any of his old girlfriends' mothers and get them pregnant either?

She needed to dig deeper into Perry Bick's past, get back on the horn to the cops in Kentucky county and double-check his story.

And she needed to find out if Clarissa Toler also had a blackmail note.

Robin reached into his pants pocket. On instinct, Winter stiffened like a statue, readying herself for anything. Instead of a weapon, he pulled out a small vape pen and took a hit.

As he blew out the white vapor, he caught Winter's wary eye. "Is this okay?" He shook the vape. "I've been trying to quit smoking, and this little bastard is the only thing that helps. I've tried everything. Gum, patches, hypnotism…"

She closed her eyes and sighed, looking for peace. This case, the flyers, and everything she'd learned from Kline that morning had her jumpier than a long-tailed cat in a room full of rocking chairs, as her Gramma Beth would say.

"Probably has something to do with my bad attitude lately." Robin pocketed the vape. "There's no nicotine in here, just something to do with my hands. I'm sorry. I've always had a bad temper."

"It's okay. I understand why you thought I was behind all this, given the flyer. It makes sense, even if it would be a very stupid and unprofitable scheme."

"No doubt." Robin squeezed his head with both hands, then stood up. "Good luck finding this asshole. If you do, give him a punch in the eye for me, huh?"

"How about you give me your contact info so I can let you know about the black eye I'll give him?" She passed him a hot-pink Post-it.

After he scrawled his cell number, Robin checked his watch and headed toward the door.

Noah followed the man, unlocked the door, and gave him a nod.

Robin slipped away without a word, and Noah locked the door behind him.

"How weird." Noah shook his head. "Where does a guy get the idea he did something like that? Drugs?"

"Maybe…" Winter shrugged, but her mind was elsewhere. *"Gum, patches, hypnotism…"*

She'd had one hypnosis session after being kidnapped and tortured by her brother. But the process hadn't done much for her. She remembered a dark room and a soft black sofa. A warm blanket. She'd talked a little bit. Mostly, though, time had taken care of things better than all of that.

"Can you hop on the computer now and start looking into Perry Bick?"

"Sure." Noah started for the desk. "What are you thinking?"

"I'm thinking it might not be a coincidence that Robin Sheen's being blackmailed for something very out of character that never even happened."

"You think Perry might be the same?"

"I don't know, but I need you to help me find out." Winter stood, drumming her fingers against her thigh. "And in the meantime, I need to investigate whether Clarissa Toler received a blackmail note too."

13

After a deliciously decadent dinner and a movie, Winter and Noah went for a drink at a fancy new bar downtown called The Red Door. A giant, monochromatic painting of Che Guevara on a tall brick wall dominated the industrial space. It was a bit much, but the ambiance was otherwise soft and subtle, with dim lighting and dark wood. They found a place on the patio, where a cool wind brushing Winter's shoulders, and browsed through a menu of thirty-seven different martinis.

Winter's stomach was still stuffed with the French onion soup and mustard-glazed short ribs she'd had for dinner, and her mind was abuzz with the new Hollywood blockbuster they'd just seen. In the vein of all modern superhero flicks, the film was a spectacle for the senses, but Noah had been predictably underwhelmed.

"It was good, but they just don't make movies the way they used to." Noah leaned back in his seat and unbuttoned the top of his shirt so she could see the barest hint of his tan skin. He'd slicked his hair back, his slacks and jacket immaculately starched and pressed. Winter was wearing a purple midi dress with a sleeveless halter that left her shoulders and the small of her back exposed.

It seemed like a thousand years since they'd gotten dressed up and gone for a night on the town. She'd even put on lashes for the occasion.

"Back in the day, they didn't feel the need to spell everything out to you. They actually expected you to think about what you were seeing."

"There's still plenty of movies like that." Winter waved a hand dismissively. "You just don't like sci-fi."

"I like superheroes, sometimes."

She rolled her eyes. "No, you don't."

"I liked that Batman movie you made me watch. You know the one. That movie expected something from its audience. It worked on a deeper level."

"Sometimes I don't want a deeper level. I just want shiny nonsense." She poked his arm. "What's wrong with that?"

"Nothing." He grabbed her hand and kissed it. "You should have all the shiny nonsense you want."

"Thank you." She grinned, but a weight was gnawing at her insides. She needed to tell Noah what had happened to Kline in Philly, needed him to know. And if she waited any longer, it would seem like she was trying to keep it from him for some reason.

Winter set her hand on Noah's knee. "I need to talk to you about something." She bit her lip. "Promise you won't freak out."

"Uh-oh."

"Maybe we should wait for our drinks…" Winter looked around the patio for their server, who had disappeared into the sea of people.

"Is it about Kline?"

She started to nod, but as she processed his question, she froze. "Why would you think it's about Kline?"

Noah pressed the tip of one finger down on the shiny black tablecloth, scrunching it, then smoothing it. "Just how he ghosted out for the rest of the day."

"He left a note."

"Have you had a chance to tell him that I'm going to be coming to work with you on a more regular basis?"

"I have not."

"I think he knows he's done all the work for you that he can at this point. I mean, you mentioned his issues on the computer. There's no way he didn't notice how painful and awkward that was."

"Oh, he definitely did."

Their drinks came. Noah had gotten himself a whiskey in a short glass with one giant square ice cube. Winter's drink was called a Japanese Slipper—glowing green liquid served up with a lemon slice and shaved cucumber. She took a sip, savoring the sweetness of Midori on her tongue. Then, before she could hesitate a moment longer, she launched into the story.

She related everything Kline had told her. The business card, the spray-painted threat on a banner, the collage of her, the sleeper hold, and waking up with no proof. As she talked, she kept her gaze on her cocktail and intermittently wiped away droplets of condensation with her fingertips.

"He thinks whoever killed Opal is coming here next, coming after me. He thinks it's all connected to Carl Gardner and Justin's fan club."

Noah's body had solidified like quick-dry concrete. He sat pole-straight in his chair, hands in his lap, whiskey untouched. "What do you think?"

"It makes sense, doesn't it? I mean, we never found out who was pulling the strings on Gardner."

"Did Kline say anything else?"

Winter swirled her drink. "Like what?"

"Like, did he say that he was afraid whoever killed Opal would be coming after him next?"

"No. I definitely got the impression that they're coming after me." Winter's voice cracked, betraying the frightened twitter of her pulse. "Whoever they are, I'm the one they want. And clearly, they don't just want to kill me. They want to scare me, break me down."

Noah sighed through his teeth. "I can't believe that son of bitch."

"Who?"

"Nothing." He pushed their drinks aside and grabbed hold of Winter's hand tightly, as though she was about to be ripped into the void.

She squeezed him back.

"I'm not going to let anything happen to you."

Winter brushed her thumb lightly over his cheek. His grimace was so dark and intense, it was painful. "I know that, baby."

"If I have to spend the rest of my life following you like a puppy, that's what I'll do. We'll get to the bottom of this."

She bit her lip and nodded. "Have you gotten anything back from Gardner's computer?"

"I doubt they've even looked at it yet."

He sounded furious, and Winter sympathized, but both of them knew how these things worked. No doubt the forensic lab had a huge backlog they had to get through, and it wasn't their job to say one case was more important than any of the others. They had to give each piece of evidence the consideration it deserved in the order it was received, unless somebody with authority put a rush on it.

"Well, in the meantime, I'm trying not to obsess about it." She didn't even want to talk about the issue now. Noah removed his jacket. His white linen shirt grazed over his chest, revealing the curve of muscle underneath. She wanted to focus on him and nothing else.

"How could you not?" He picked up his whiskey but still didn't drink. "I can't believe it took Kline so long to tell you this."

"Yeah, I'm not exactly thrilled about that either."

"He should've called us the minute it happened. I mean, this is your life we're talking about."

"I'm so sick of being on guard all the time." Winter blew out an exasperated breath. "I flinch at everything. I can never relax. You should feel the damn knots in my back."

Noah lifted one eyebrow. "I think a proper back rub would be the perfect way to end this evening." He hooked a hand under her chair and slid it about six inches closer.

She smiled in spite of herself. He hadn't even touched her shoulders yet, and she already felt better.

He leaned forward, locking his eyes with her in a way that told her he had something to share. "Sometimes, I feel like I'm back in Iraq." He finally took a sip from his glass. "Like people are hunting me and the people I care about twenty-four seven. I can never relax, always gotta keep my guard up. It's running down my battery, and I know it's draining yours."

"I feel more like a rabbit or a squirrel. Everything's trying to eat me, so I'm always on alert, wide-eyed and twitching."

"Leave it to you to make it sound cute." He leaned in and kissed her forehead.

"It's not cute. It's beyond exhausting." She pushed her drink away, folded her arms on the table, and laid her head on top. "I feel like I've been waiting my whole life for it to be over, but it just goes on and on."

"What does, babe?" Noah placed a hand lovingly on the middle of her back.

"Stress. The constant worry that somebody might jump

out any minute and try to kill me or you." She sighed again, sinking deeper into the table. "Fake flyers. Fake memories. It all has to be connected."

"I can't help but wonder if this has more to do with Kline than we realize."

Winter wrinkled her nose and peered up into her husband's forest-green eyes. "What do you mean?"

"I mean, you weren't connected to Opal. Not really. If this person is just trying to screw with you, it'd make more sense to go after someone you're close to. Like me or Ariel or Gramma Beth and Grampa Jack."

"Maybe he's working up to it." Winter clenched her eyes shut and shook her head. "I couldn't bear it—"

"We're not going to let that happen." Noah brushed her hair aside. "Darlin'?"

She looked up at him.

"We won't let that happen."

"I'm glad you're so confident. You can be confident for both of us."

"Maybe it'd be best if Kline left. Hit the road again, like he does." Noah took another sip of his whiskey, his eyes searching her face over his glass. "He's done everything he can for you."

Winter didn't answer right away. She and Kline had bonded somewhat, but despite their shared DNA, they were still strangers. She wondered if they always would be. So much time had passed—her whole life gone by, never knowing her biological father. Maybe it didn't matter anymore.

She wasn't even sure if she would feel sad if he left. Having him in the office and trying to find things for him to do was nothing but stressful, let alone how odd it felt when he stayed at her house.

But if he left and the killer went after him, she'd never forgive herself.

"I guess," she said at last. "But either way, I'll make a point to talk to him tomorrow. I have to go to the station anyway. I'll convince him to come with me so he can fess up to identity fraud. We can't have that coming between you and me or all of us any longer."

Noah brushed her hair away from her eyes. He seemed relieved she was finally going to do the right thing and maybe a little sad too. It was hard to tell in the dim lighting.

"I'm tired." Winter sat up, finished off her drink, and took a bite of the lemon slice. "Let's go home."

14

When Winter and Noah went into the office the next morning, they found a note taped to the front door. Winter's guard immediately went up. But when she ripped it down, she recognized Kline's handwriting.

If I could go back in time, I would stay at your mother's side. I would hold you in my arms as a baby. I would watch you grow. I would protect you from everything that ever tried to hurt you. But it's too late for that. All I can give you now is one less thing to worry about.

Please don't try to find me. Just trust that it's better this way.

Your father loves you. Now and forever.

Tears welled in Winter's eyes, but they didn't fall. She read the note again, pressing a hand over her mouth. She wasn't sure how she was supposed to feel. Sad? Angry? Betrayed?

Relieved?

All of that and none of it at once. Her body was so drawn up with emotion, it was getting harder to breathe. He came into her life without warning, and now he was gone just as quickly. The father she never knew. Never would know.

She was angry. That was it. He'd blown into her life and blown back out at his convenience. Kline was a coward. Their relationship had been awkward since his confession, but that would've passed.

She'd tried to teach him how to use a computer yesterday. She clearly wanted him to stay. Her heart had grown attached. And now her head was pissed. Did he love her *now and forever*? She doubted the man even knew what that meant.

"What is it?" Noah was quick with a hand on her shoulder.

She let her head fall heavily against his chest. "It's Kline. He's gone." For as angry as she was, she had no fight to release, just a heavy sigh of disappointment mixed with the very familiar feeling of heartbreak over another lost family member.

Tightening his hand around her waist, he gently ushered her through the door and locked it behind them. "I'm sorry."

"How could he just leave like that? Without even saying goodbye." She sniffled, realizing a tear or two had fallen, only to be absorbed by Noah's shirt. Winter looked up at her husband and shook her head, the tingles in her eyes slowly subsiding. "I guess he left a note. That's more than usual."

"Did he say where he's gone?"

"Very much no. He clearly doesn't want anything to do with me." She passed him the note. "Who could blame him? Everywhere I go, people end up murdered. If we'd never reconnected, Opal would probably still be alive."

"Don't go down that path, please. That isn't your fault. And remember, he came looking for you."

Winter sank into the chair behind the reception desk and rested her chin in her hands.

No, she wasn't going to pity herself. Noah was right. Kline's reasons for leaving were his reasons. Heck, he wasn't even Kline Hurst. She hadn't yet begun to know her biological father and couldn't possibly come to any conclusions about why he up and left.

Noah set his hands on the desk and peered down at her. "Darlin', Kline told me yesterday that he was planning on leaving."

"What?" She sat up straight. "Why didn't you tell me?"

"He told me he wanted a chance to tell you himself. If I knew that meant leaving a damn note on your door…" He rubbed his face. "I'm sorry. I thought he was going to have a heart-to-heart with you."

"That's not his style, I guess." She raked her fingers through her hair. Noah believed the man just yesterday about his intentions to tell her goodbye in person. He'd even convinced Noah to keep his departure from her. This was all the proof she needed to realize she truly did not know Kline and neither did her husband.

"It's fine, babe. I'm glad you gave him a chance to say goodbye in his own way. If that's just to disappear."

Noah set the note down on the desk in front of her. She twirled it with one finger, scanning the words again.

It's too late for that.

Neither of them had been ready or willing to open up in the way it took to really be a family. He'd always be a vagabond, and she'd always be…what was she? She was an orphan.

No.

She was a woman who wasn't raised by parents in the traditional sense but who had survived, nonetheless. And she'd survived being tortured and kidnapped and worse. She was currently surviving who knew how many stalkers. She'd found the love of a damn good man, and together, they'd created their own kind of family.

And she would handle whatever lay ahead with those fake flyers.

She couldn't control Kline, but she could control her own emotions, and this hiccup wouldn't bring her down. She inhaled deeply, held it in for four long seconds, and breathed it all out.

"In a way, I guess I'm relieved. Is that horrible to say?"

"No. Of course not. He's a big boy. You did everything you could for him. You're not responsible for his life."

"I know."

Noah gave her a side hug and headed back toward the door. Picking up the note, Winter held it to her chest and smiled sadly. "Goodbye, Kline. Good luck."

A pile of mail lay on the floor beneath the mail slot. Noah scooped it up and headed to the little recycling bin, standing over it as he sorted through the papers.

His whole body stiffened. "Oh, shit."

"What?"

Noah walked back to the desk and dropped the mail in front of her. Immediately, Winter recognized the fake flyer, just like the other three.

Fumbling through Ariel's desk drawers until she found some disposable gloves, Winter pulled them on and picked up the flyer. Nothing special distinguished it from the others. And there was no stamp, so she knew it had been hand delivered.

"The cameras—"

"I'm on it." Noah went into Winter's office and switched on her computer.

Winter read the flyer and set it aside. A letter written with cutout newspaper and magazine type was waiting for her underneath it.

Ding dong, your aunt is dead. The time to level up is over, Winter. I'm coming.

The Listener.

She deposited the note into its own bag and stood staring at it, dread curdling in her stomach.

"The system's loading." Noah came back to the desk and leaned over her shoulder, reading the letter himself. "It's different from the others. Why bother with the old magazine trick? Why not just type it out like the rest?"

"Because he's not blackmailing me." Winter chewed the inside of her cheek. "He's singling me out. He wants me to know his beef with me is different. Bigger."

"Do you think the person sending these flyers and the blackmail letters is the same one who killed Opal? The one who left the message for Kline?"

The question chilled her blood. That connection had been buzzing around the back of her brain like flies on rotten fruit. "He's playing a game. I think all this is for my sake." She waved her gloved hand over the notes on her desk. "The banner. Opal. All of it. Everyone else is just collateral damage."

"And the flyers?"

She lifted her shoulders, shivering from the chill in the air. "It's his way of inviting me to play with him. And this letter is his way of saying player two has officially entered the game."

"I think it's time we go to APD with all this."

Winter nodded. "You're right. We can't keep trying to handle this on our own."

"One nice thing about being in the FBI, you're never really alone. You always have your team."

"At least I have you now." Winter removed her glove and pulled out her phone.

"Can you get ahold of Davenport?"

"Darnell's in New Mexico working to extradite a murder suspect back to Texas. But I'll touch base with Detective

Lessner. He's the one who's working Clarissa Toler's case. She was the first one to receive a flyer." Winter scrolled down to Lessner's cell number and paused. "I wonder if she was being blackmailed too. If that was the reason she did what she did."

She'd had the idea on her list of things to investigate. Now would be a good time to check off that item.

"If the Listener's the same person who killed Opal, then it makes me think Clarissa Toler could've been killed by them too." Noah's jaw tightened. "And Perry and Robin and any others who might've received these flyers could be in a lot of danger."

"You're right. I'll contact them too." She pressed the button to call Lessner and put the phone to her ear. In her office, her computer made the happy sound of awakening, and Noah hurried off to check the security footage.

15

The security cameras showed a figure dressed in black with a black hood and a ski mask delivering the letter just after midnight. And with the way they crouched and shuffled, darting into frame for less than a second before darting out again, it was impossible to tell height or gender. The figure had a thin or medium build. It wasn't much to go on.

Winter was relieved they at least had the cameras set up, but Noah threw a tantrum about it. The only camera to capture an image of the Listener was one Kline installed—up too high to be any use. He cursed Kline for being incompetent and cursed himself for trusting him.

He stayed behind at the office to fix the problem and wait for Perry or Robin to call back while Winter headed back downtown for yet another meeting with Detective Lessner.

At the police station, Winter was left to wait for nearly an hour before Detective Lessner deigned to see her. Eventually, the short, squat, perpetually grimacing cop led her into an interview room and invited her to sit across from him at a table.

Winter tried for exactly eight seconds before giving up on

the idea. She'd already been sitting for too long while she'd waited for the detective, and her body was charged like a transformer ready to burst. She shot out of her seat and moved around the room—pacing, stretching, touching the cold brick walls—as she presented her story and her evidence.

"It's different from the others." Winter pointed at the threatening note that sat on the wooden table in front of the detective. "And given every blackmail note came with one of these bogus flyers, I think it's safe to assume I'm the real target, don't you agree?"

"Maybe." Lessner rubbed his index finger over his temple. He looked tired and irritated. Winter reminded herself that cops often looked like that in general and tried not to take it personally. "It's safe to assume the blackmail demands and the flyers originated from the same source."

"The Listener." She raked her fingers through her hair in frustration. "But what exactly could they be listening to if the memories are false? Was Clarissa Toler being blackmailed too?"

"That's privileged information."

Winter bumped to a stop. "Are you kidding me? I work with this department all the time. I'm being targeted. I don't know if you're aware of the Carl Gardner case—"

"I am."

"Then you understand how deep all of this might go."

"You're frightened. It's understandable." He took a painfully slow slurp from his coffee mug. "That fear's causing you to leap to conclusions."

Winter's teeth clenched so tight, they made a horrible scratchy noise. "I haven't come to any conclusions. I'm just trying to get a handle on the evidence. Detective Davenport is—"

"Detective Davenport is not the lead on the Clarissa Toler case."

"So it's an open case? Does that mean the M.E. didn't rule it a suicide?"

"We have no indication that Clarissa Toler was a victim of foul play."

"But you won't tell me if she was being blackmailed?"

"Here's what I'm going to do." Lessner stretched his hands out over the notes. "I'll send all these to the lab with the others and see if we can pull any prints off them."

She nodded along, but her teeth were still clenched. "Someone's trying to hurt me, or drive me crazy, or both. Someone's been watching me for months. Now somebody's sending specific people my way, people who are being blackmailed. And the person sending the blackmail letters sent me a taunting letter about my murdered aunt…"

"I understand why you're upset." Detective Lessner took another sip of coffee, his demeanor frustratingly calm.

"I'm not upset." Winter slammed both palms down on the table. "I'm fucking terrified. My aunt was murdered. Somebody ambushed her and stabbed her over a dozen times, an old woman who never hurt anybody. And the fact that we were related wasn't exactly common knowledge. I only found out myself a few weeks before she died."

Lessner's expression remained unchanged. Tired, irritated. She wanted to punch him in the face.

Instead, she pulled back and kept pacing. "The only way we even found each other is because somebody contacted her, pretending to be my friend. Somebody stole my DNA and submitted it to an online genealogy database."

He typed a few notes on his open laptop, but the amble of his clicking fingers indicated a casual approach to the situation.

"I'm not a conspiracy theorist, okay? And I don't think

I'm at the center of every case. I'm an investigator. I collect and interpret evidence." She pushed her hand through her hair. "And though I desperately want to deny it, the evidence strongly suggests all this is connected. The Listener, my aunt's murder, Carl Gardner, and the surveillance cameras we found posted outside my grandparents' home and my office." Winter forced herself to take a deep breath, shorter on the inhale and longer on the exhale.

"Here's what I'll do. I'll contact the homicide investigators in Philadelphia." Lessner sorted through the evidence bags Winter had brought, picking up the one containing the business card Kline had given her, the one with the address of an abandoned house written on the back in angry block letters. "I'll make sure they comb through the house. If it really was done up the way you said, there's a good chance evidence was left behind. Maybe we'll be able to find something."

"Thank you." The meagerest amount of tension released from Winter's shoulders.

"I'll put a rush on testing the papers for fingerprints. If the Listener is as dangerous as you think, then we've got much bigger problems. Anybody who's received one of these letters might be in serious danger."

Winter left the police station feeling somehow worse than when she'd gone in. It was the first time she'd said all of that out loud, admitting to herself the possible, or even probable, extent of the conspiracy against her.

And she couldn't help thinking that was the reason Kline left. Not because he'd done enough. Not because he didn't see a future for their relationship. He left because being close to Winter was dangerous. It always had been. So many people had been hurt simply for knowing her. Kline saw firsthand what happened to his sister, who'd never even met Winter in person. He left because he feared he might be next.

She couldn't blame him. Sometimes, she wished she could do the same.

When she arrived back at the office, Noah was sitting at Ariel's desk, tapping away at the keyboard. Except it wasn't Ariel's desk anymore. Noah had removed the little golden touch lamp, the tiny succulent in a kitten-shaped pot, the purple cosmic-swirl desk mat.

It was Noah's desk now, with no knickknacks but plenty of pens scattered around. His black water bottle sat perilously close to the computer keyboard. Without a replacement, he was stuck with Ariel's pastel-pink one.

Otherwise, it was fairly neat. A stack of papers sat in a tidy pile off to the side. Maybe he'd learned a few organization tricks from his previous SSAs. He needed to make himself at home while he was there, but something about the way he cleared out Ariel's stuff without even asking irked Winter. Ariel wasn't gone for good. She'd be back.

Hopefully.

"You were right," he said when she walked in. "You're always right."

Those words were exactly what she needed to hear at that moment. Not because they fed her ego, but because talking to Lessner left her feeling like she was losing her mind. Having someone like Noah—a man who by all accounts had everything together—tell her she not only wasn't crazy but was absolutely right restored her faith in a universe that made sense.

She walked to him and draped her body over his shoulder, pressing her cheek to his and inhaling his cologne. "What was I right about?"

"Perry. He lied to you."

Winter furrowed her brow and pulled herself to a stand. "Tell me."

"Well, first of all, he didn't even go to Eastern Kentucky University during the time he claims he beat a guy into a coma. He was there for his first semester, and he was seventeen until mid-November. He wasn't even old enough to work in a bar or club. Then he left the first week in December after finals, never to return. He transferred to Vanderbilt, the school he graduated from."

Winter folded her arms. "That's a very strange thing to lie about."

"I found pictures of him during his college years. He was the co-president of a finance club, and he volunteered in the local food pantry. I even found an alumni website where he's friends with a bunch of other folks who attended Vanderbilt with him. I verified his enrollment dates with EKU and Vanderbilt."

Exhausted and with a dull throb in the back of her brain, Winter sank down into the little white chair beside the desk. "And the strip club?"

Noah shook his head. "Perry worked in the library and part time at a pizza place. I couldn't find anything to indicate he had another job, and frankly, with his time already split six different ways, I don't know how it would even be possible." He nodded toward the computer. "Most importantly, I checked records for a month on either side of the date he gave you all over Kentucky and Tennessee, and there are no reports of anyone being beaten into a coma outside any strip club."

"That's damn good work."

Noah bobbed his eyebrows. "Not to brag, but I have done this kind of thing once or twice."

Winter leaned back in her chair and popped her neck. "I don't get it. How the hell do you blackmail someone over something that never even happened? And how do you get someone to remember something that isn't true to even get to the point of blackmailing?"

"It seems a lot more likely that they're both lying. Maybe Perry Bick and Robin Sheen are in this together. Maybe they're screwing with you."

She studied the hardwood floor, her gaze following the twists and flaws on turns in the pretty boards. "Maybe."

"You don't think so."

"I don't know what I think. Not yet. Has either one called the office?"

Noah glanced at the landline on Robin's desk. None of the lights indicating waiting messages were lit. "Doesn't look like it."

Winter took out her phone and scrolled through the contacts 'til she found Perry Bick to try him again. The phone rang several times. She thought it was about to go to voicemail when he finally picked up.

"Hello?"

"Hi, Perry. It's Winter Black. We had an appointment. I need to talk to you about your case and go over your story again. Could you come down to the office? It's urgent."

"Umm…I don't think so. I can talk on the phone."

"I'd rather speak to you in person."

"Okay…" His words came out with a singsong note of hesitation. "You can come to where I am."

Winter snatched one of Noah's haphazard pens off the desk, as well as the pad of hot-pink sticky notes. "What's the address?"

16

Even before I became interested in neuroscience and the ways the human brain could be manipulated through hypnotism, I was fascinated by the dynamics of trust and affection. It was surprisingly simple to get another person to like you, to convince them to ignore gigantic red flags.

Smiling, laughing at their jokes, asking them questions they desperately wanted to answer—these actions led to affection, and affection led to trust. Finding ways to run into a person unexpectedly, and in different environments, also opened them up.

That was how trust was reciprocated. I started running into my subjects in other environments, too, and the opportunity to really study my interest blossomed. To discover what they thought was missing in their lives and find some small way to fulfill it.

The bond always developed from there. I took care not to open up too much, so I wasn't exposed to counterattack. I would pick one solid story. That was all it ever took. Then my subjects would sing like canaries.

I knew just what to say to elevate them. And once they felt more self-assured, I knew how to devalue them. I saw right into their vulnerability, and that was how I obtained the information I needed to mold my subject as I saw fit.

Once that was achieved, our relationship remained in this parasitic state until I was ready to discard them. Normally, this cycle took months or years, but it could be accelerated with the right complementary tools.

Such as hypnotism.

Now, this kind of manipulation could also be used to obtain sexual gratification. Con artists and grifters used similar tactics to gain money from their victims. And there were times when I'd found myself short on cash or even strangely drawn to another person to the point where I desired to conquer them—and did. But lately, this skill set had come in handy in my professional working environment exclusively.

The work I was doing now was the convergence of all my pain, my studies, and my ambitions. My path had led me to this opportunity, a place where I could finally avenge my past. This experiment would prove my crowning achievement.

Hypnotism was all about trust. To truly hypnotize a person and gain access to their subconscious, I had to plant dozens of little anchors of trust in their minds. They had to believe with all their heart that I would do them no harm. They had to believe I'd keep their secrets.

That was the true work of a hypnotist, working on the conscious mind like a bank robber cracked a safe. And once I got inside, planting a false memory was easy enough to do. Changing the way a person felt and responded to stimuli was even easier.

Men, I had found, were especially susceptible. They

skated along the surface of their own selves, clueless and overconfident and, therefore, too trusting of the opposite sex—which some still viewed as inferior, despite it being the twenty-first century. Those were my favorite subjects.

Speaking of…

Confident though I was that I had a handle on what needed to be done, every day I grew more worried about the partner I'd chosen. All my life, I'd been a dormant powder keg, but Erik was the spark. He was a doer, not someone who spent all his time learning and ruminating, as I had a tendency to do. But did that mean I trusted him?

Not even a little.

I first met him in a dark corner of the internet, in a community with axes to grind. People who'd endured trauma and injustice. People who weren't trying to "let go" of their desire for vengeance—to heal themselves and find peace, as the popular narrative prescribed. We were a group of individuals looking for catharsis and trying to figure out how to get it.

Erik was different. The others were more like me. Wounded animals too frightened and too indoctrinated by society to do anything beyond whining online to other whiners. We lacked the bravery to take the first step. That was what Erik did for me.

Our stories of woe didn't really matter. Erik was not the pitying type. Instead, we focused on talking about our respective targets. His was Winter Black. And mine, as it turned out, lived right in Austin too.

Eventually, we moved our conversation from the dark web to the telephone. I hadn't known what to expect, but his energy alarmed me at first. It didn't take long to realize why he was brave enough to pull the trigger when most of us were not…

He was completely off his rocker.

Erik suffered from antisocial personality disorder. I didn't judge him for that. I had the same condition. It was what made me so adept at what I did. No pointless empathy getting in the way of my plans.

But there was something more with Erik. Something unpredictable about his behavior that had nothing to do with his distaste for people. I told myself not to think about it or panic over the wild horse I'd hitched my apple cart to.

We decided to start meeting in person. One night, we got very drunk together, and I mentioned my degree in psychology and cognitive science and my intimate knowledge of manipulation and hypnotism.

Erik was enthralled. He asked all the right questions. He validated me in a way no one ever had before.

He came to me with a plan for both of us to achieve the catharsis we sought. I didn't understand his idea or his motivation, but I knew the small role he wanted me to play was the missing link to my own success. So I readily accepted his offer to join forces.

But when all this was done, I feared that getting rid of Erik would be a problem. To proactively ensure his eventual, um, *dismissal* would be smooth, I was attaching my anchors, laying my foundation, and getting his soft mind ready for takeover.

My phone buzzed in my pocket. I didn't have to look to know who it was—and it wasn't even lunchtime yet. High-maintenance Erik. Calling and texting constantly, wanting to be updated on every little step I took, even after I'd informed him that last night went off seamlessly. Meanwhile, I was the one doing all the damn work. Sure, he came up with the plan. But since then, he'd sat back like a general on a hilltop, shouting orders at me.

I couldn't wait to be rid of him. But I had to be patient. I still needed him for now. And if something went wrong, and I found myself under the hot lights of police scrutiny, he was my escape plan.

My sacrificial lamb.

17

Arriving at Lakeview Hills Memorial Hospital, Winter checked in with security and paused at the nurse's station to ask directions to Perry Bick's hospital room. The sterile smell in the air wrapped around her like wet wool, weighing down her steps.

She'd never been a fan of hospitals. Too many memories of times when she'd failed to protect the people who depended on her.

When she entered a tiny room stuffed to the gills with heart monitors and other beeping machines, she focused on Perry lying in the hospital bed. The tan Adonis who had come seeking her help had faded—pale, haggard, and weak. His wrists were wrapped in thick white bandages.

"Hello," was all she could think to say.

He replied with a weak smile.

A nurse who'd accompanied her went to his bedside and checked a few machines. He touched the mostly empty IV bag and marked something in his chart before drifting from the room.

Winter stepped closer, turned sideways so as not to

disturb any equipment, and took a seat on the round, backless rolling stool beside the bed. "I don't understand. Why did you do it?"

He glanced toward her without lifting his face before turning toward the opposite wall. "They gave me a choice. A way to pay for what I did. I don't have thirty grand lying around. I tried to come up with it. I sold my car. I went to my bank to get a loan."

"Oh, Perry." She sighed and rubbed her eyes with one hand.

"So I got the loan. Then I went online, and I made myself a Paymo account. I was going to pay this guy off, but then…"

"You had a change of heart?"

"This voice in my head just kept saying this was the only way out."

Winter knew all too well about intrusive thoughts, but voices were something else entirely. She wondered if Perry's really were in his head, but she'd come here for other answers first and had to prioritize.

His shaking hands clenched the thin blanket. "It's not enough for what I did. He might not have technically died, but I still took a man's life. I deserve to pay for it. An eye for an eye."

Winter flinched as little cracks formed in her heart. Noah's theory about Robin Sheen and Perry Bick had almost made sense until this moment. But nobody was this good of a liar, this committed to a nonsense story. She was sure Perry believed every word he was saying.

"I know this is about the last thing you want to talk about right now, but did you write that statement I asked for? The description of everything you remembered from that night?"

"I tried." He tipped his head back and looked up at the ceiling. "I don't have anything more to tell you. I already said what happened. Nobody else was there that night. Nobody saw anything."

"Let's just go over it one more time." Winter didn't want to let on just yet what she had learned from the Kentucky authorities, and she didn't want to explain that she'd stopped combing through the details, trying to get a fix on a blackmailer. If she simply told Perry that what he remembered wasn't the truth, she sensed he would dismiss her. But maybe she could show him.

"You worked in a strip club in Madison County when you were a student putting yourself through college. One night in December, a man was harassing you, so you got into a physical altercation where you beat him so badly that he slipped into a coma from which he has yet to wake up."

"Exactly." Perry pursed his lips, the skin around his eyes wrinkling in pain. "So what the hell else do you want to know?"

"Please, it's important. You have to believe that I have nothing but your interests at heart. I'm trying to get to the bottom of this, but I need your help."

"I don't care anymore." He inhaled sharply, a scrape of tears in his throat. "It doesn't matter."

"I assure you that it does matter. You're not the only one being targeted by the Listener. You have a chance right now to help someone else. Isn't that worth going over the story again?"

His bloodshot eyes softened. He flattened the blanket on his lap. "It was my sophomore year."

She set the trap. "At Vanderbilt, right?"

Perry nodded, the phantom of a grin flashing at the corner of his lips. "Yeah. Vanderbilt University, home of the Commodores."

Gotcha.

Winter bit back a satisfied smile. At last, she was getting

somewhere. His story was changing completely. "And you were how old?"

"I'd just turned nineteen."

"Go on."

"I needed some extra money, so I was working at a strip club in a nearby town. One night, a guy followed me and was harassing me, shouting all these homophobic things and spitting on me. I fought him. I beat him up. He's still in a coma." Perry cradled his head in his hands, sobbing dry tears. His chest seemed hollow as he gasped to try to pull himself together.

"What was the man's name?"

Perry shook his head, pressing his thumbs into his eyes to push out his tears. "I don't know."

"Then how do you know he's still in a coma?"

"I just…I check on him. I've called the hospital."

"Which hospital?"

"I can't remember. He's in Richmond."

"Virginia?"

"Kentucky. Near EKU where I went to school."

Winter pressed her lips together and folded them in. She waited to see if he would notice what he'd just said.

A liar would've realized such an obvious mistake in their story, but Perry was consumed with the emotion of it. Even if the narrative was nonsense, the way he felt about it was as real as anything.

"What was your stage name?"

He shook his head. "I don't remember. It was so long ago."

"What was the name of the pizza place where you worked?"

"Petey's Pies."

"How did you pay off your student loans?"

He pounded the mattress next to his thigh. "What the hell does that have to do with anything?"

"Please, just answer. I'll explain everything, I promise."

"I was mostly on scholarship. When I got my first market analysis job out of college, I kept living like a student and paid off my loans within that first year."

"And the money you made stripping?"

"Yeah, that helped a lot."

"You used it to pay off your loans?"

"A big chunk of it, I think. Yeah."

"At the club, were there more men or women?"

"Uh…" Perry fiddled with a loose string on the blanket, rolling it into a little ball and then pulling it straight. "Pretty even mix, I guess."

"What did most patrons come for, the alcohol or the entertainers?"

"I don't know. Both. The alcohol. No. Definitely the dancers." He rubbed his temple, then slapped both his hands down in frustration. "What is this all about?"

"What was the most popular pizza at Petey's Pies?"

"The New York style pepperoni. They also had a White Cheesy people went nuts for." He smiled nostalgically. "And the calzones were a hit. They were the size of a fat baby."

"The man you beat up. What did he look like?"

He stared at the wall, as if willing to see the guy's face appear. "I don't know. He was just a man. He looked like a man."

"Was he white? Black? Was he tall? What was his build?"

"It was dark. I don't remember."

"Was Petey's Pies owned by a guy named Petey?"

"Yeah."

"What did he look like?"

"He was just a fat Italian dude. He had a handlebar mustache. He was going bald." A bead of sweat ran down his temple. "What do you want from me? What does this have to do with anything?"

Winter sat back in her chair, drumming her fingers on her knee. She thought of Robin Sheen and his own confused memories. She thought of his vape pen and his twitchy fingers.

"Do you see a therapist, Perry?"

He drew his head back on his neck, thrown off by the question. "Yeah. I do. I've been going once a week for a while now. Why?"

"What do you work on with your therapist?"

"I have anxiety and depression. I was diagnosed with ADHD a while back. We've been working on my executive functioning and time management."

"What kind of therapy do you do together? Talk analysis?"

"Yeah, a little. But my therapist specializes in neurofeedback and hypnosis. She gets deep into your brain to help reprogram some of the unhelpful stuff."

Unhelpful, such as smoking? Nicotine's a pretty unhelpful habit that Robin Sheen's trying to break through hypnosis.

Winter's whole body tingled, and she sat up straight. "Have you ever talked to your therapist about the incident with the man in the coma?"

"I don't think so." He looked genuinely confused, more so than before. "But we must have."

"Perry, I need to tell you something, and it's going to sound crazy." Winter reached out and placed her hand on the edge of the hospital bed. "Before I do, I want you to know that this isn't just a theory. It's backed by considerable evidence and your own, albeit unintentional, testimony."

He almost looked afraid for her to continue. "What are you talking about?"

"You never worked at a strip club."

His eyes widened, and he laughed uncomfortably. "Yeah, I did. I told you I did."

"No. You didn't. You went to Eastern Kentucky University for how long?"

"Just one semester, and then I transferred. Vanderbilt had a better program in my field."

"Okay, so how could you work at a strip club at age seventeen?"

"It was my sophomore year. I was nineteen in December, when this happened."

She lowered her tone and slowed down her pacing. "It didn't happen because you lived in Nashville then. You never worked at a strip club. And you didn't beat a guy so badly he ended up in a coma. None of this ever happened."

"Yes, I did." Perry's cheeks flushed, and his eyes misted over. "Why are you messing with me? You're not making me feel better."

"Perry, I'm not your mom. I don't care about making you feel better. I know what you remember seems real, but the human brain is capable of being convinced of all kinds of untruths." She took a deep breath. "I know it's confusing, but I think somebody implanted these memories in your head specifically so they could blackmail you over them."

He stared at her as if she'd sprouted a second head. "Implanted them? I don't even know what that means."

"Via hypnosis. It's rare, but it's not unheard of. While in a hypnotic state, it's easy to blur the lines between fact and fiction. I have a lot more investigating to do, but my working theory is that you were targeted and made to believe you did something horrible."

"Why would anybody do that?"

Winter had been asking herself the same question. The only logical answer was the one provided by Clarissa Toler, even if Lessner refused to help her confirm the theory.

"Whoever it was, I think they were trying to get you to kill yourself."

He covered his face with his hands. "You're wrong. It's so real. I remember the blood. I remember—"

"Take it from someone who has taken another human life." She pressed her palm flat over her chest. "Traumatic memories are often out of order and confusing. Sometimes they're missing entirely. And sometimes you vividly remember things that did not happen."

He lifted his eyes to her, trembling with fear and confusion. "I don't understand. What's happening to me?"

"I'm going to do everything I can to answer that question. And you're going to help me, right?"

He nodded, but the movement slowly transformed into a headshake. "What help can I be if I don't even know what's going on in my own head?"

"What's your therapist's name?"

"Why do you want to know that?"

Winter didn't want to answer that question in earnest. Not yet. But she also didn't want to outright lie to the poor, confused man. "If nothing else, they might be able to help us understand what's real and what isn't."

"Dr. Ava Poole at the Blue Tree Wellness Center. She's helped me a lot. Or at least, I thought she had."

"I'm sure she has." Winter set her hand lightly on his arm. "I'm going to get to the bottom of this. But I need you to do something for me."

"What?" His voice was so weak, fading like a star fleeing the rising sun.

"Don't lose hope."

18

Winter leaned over Noah's shoulder as he clicked the link to the Blue Tree Wellness Center's website. *Discover Healing, Find Balance, Embrace Wellness.*

When she'd returned to the office to relay what Perry had told her, Noah said he'd gotten ahold of Robin Sheen, who irritably and with a lot of volume confirmed he also received hypnotherapy at the same place, from the same doctor.

As he scrolled down, Winter scanned through the website copy. Nothing she wouldn't expect to find on any therapy center's main page. Affirmations about the transformative power of healing, a laundry list of their therapists' qualifications, a promise of personalized and holistic care.

She paused over a paragraph describing the range of therapies. *From massage therapy to cognitive behavioral therapy, acupuncture to nutrition counseling, movement therapy and EMDR to neurofeedback and hypnosis, we offer a broad spectrum of therapeutic modalities to suit your unique health needs.*

The center comprised a group of practitioners working both as individuals and as a group that offered referrals to one another to match clients with different modalities. From the photos, it looked like a wellness campus filled with various bland brick office buildings. Noah clicked on the menu link *About Us*, which opened a secondary menu listing each of the individual therapists and doctors by name.

Dr. Ava Poole.

Noah opened her bio. She was a pale woman in her mid- to late fifties with long white hair. She had a long face and curious, wide set eyes that made her look like a praying mantis, and a smile that was understated but alluring.

"'As a seasoned psychologist,'" Noah read out loud, "'Dr. Ava Poole has honed her skills in two transformative therapeutic modalities, eye movement desensitization and reprocessing and hypnosis therapy. EMDR is a highly effective method for processing traumatic experiences, while hypnosis allows individuals to access their inner resources and make positive changes at a subconscious level. Dr. Poole's expertise enables her to offer a comprehensive and holistic approach to mental health and emotional well-being.'"

Her degrees and professional certificates were all listed at the bottom. She'd earned her Doctorate of Psychology from UCLA.

"She seems perfectly respectable, don't you think?"

Winter nodded, but that didn't mean too much to her. She'd known far too many respectable people with blood-soaked skeletons in their closets.

"What are you thinking, darlin'?"

"I'm thinking I need to ask Robin Sheen the name of the doctor administering his hypnosis therapy. And find out if Clarissa Toler might have been a patient as well." Winter tapped her finger to her lips. "We haven't created any boards to find a true connection with these three cases, but this might be it."

"It's a powerful coincidence, I'll give you that. Two people being blackmailed over wrongs they remember committing that never actually happened."

"And if the same world-class expert in hypnosis just happens to have both of them as patients…" Winter reached over his shoulder and clicked through the website until she found the office address. She typed it into her phone's map app. "I'm going to head down to talk to Dr. Poole myself."

"I'll come with you."

Winter kissed his cheek. "I won't be long. I need you to track down Robin and ask him about his therapist. He seems more analytical than Perry, less trusting and emotional. He might be able to give us more useful information." She squeezed Noah's shoulder. "And while you're at it, you could do some more digging into Dr. Poole. I can't help feeling she's not as squeaky clean as she'd have us believe."

❄

Stepping into Blue Tree Wellness Center was like walking into a high-end spa. Gray marble tiles covered the floor, and beautiful hand fans in muted natural colors adorned a wall opposite a fountain of copper and stone. A woman sat behind an ornate desk with living bamboo paneling. The air smelled vaguely of frankincense, and the rhythmic beats of meditation music played gently in the background.

An older woman in a pink tracksuit stood at the desk, speaking in harsh tones to the receptionist. "You tell Dr. Poole she better call me soon. If not, she's going to have a lot more to worry about than a few broken appointments."

She turned and grimaced, marching out without an upward glance.

Winter's boots squeaked as she approached the desk. The scowl on the receptionist's face flipped into a friendly, close-lipped smile when she spotted Winter. She was petite, with black hair cut at her shoulders and baby bangs. Her large eyes were so dark, light seemed to fall into them. Her skin was pale with no warmth of blush. A placard on the desk displayed her name. *Cybil Kerie.*

"Hello, I'm Cybil. How can I help you?"

"Hi. I'm here to speak with Dr. Poole."

"Do you have an appointment?"

Winter shook her head and lightly ran the tip of her fingers over the bamboo growing in front of the desk. "I'm here on a personal matter. If she could spare just a few minutes, it would be very much appreciated."

"Umm." Cybil put a short but well-manicured fingernail on her bottom lip. "She's booked this afternoon, but she might be willing to speak with you on her break between appointments. I'll ask her when she's finished with the current session, if you'd like to wait."

"Thank you." Winter took a seat in one of the waiting chairs—soft and squishy and so comfortable, she was tempted to rest her head back and close her eyes.

"Might I get you anything to drink?" Cybil stepped out from behind her desk. She was a tiny woman, no more than five feet tall and with bones like a bird. "Water, sparkling water, coffee, tea?"

"Water would be great, thank you."

Cybil left the room, and Winter nabbed a few of Dr. Ava Poole's business cards and pocketed them before the receptionist returned with a frosted glass bottle. She handed it to Winter and returned to her desk.

Winter cracked open the lid and took a deep drink. "Have you been working here long?"

"About three months now, I guess."

"Do you like it?"

"It's a great place to work. The mental health benefits can't be beat."

Winter smiled at the joke. "Are you very interested in mental health?"

"Oh, yes." Cybil's cool face brightened. "I've always been fascinated by the human mind and neuroscience. Why we do what we do."

"So have I, in a different discipline. I imagine you'd be interested in working as a therapist?"

Winter planned to chitchat at first before warming up to the questions she really wanted answers to.

"Someday, absolutely, when I get a string of letters after my name. I do a lot of volunteer work for now."

"What do you think of Dr. Poole's approach?"

Cybil's face drooped a bit. "I think it's uncommon. Hypnosis isn't something a lot of doctors specialize in."

"Why do you think that is?"

"Because it has a bad reputation, for one. And what they say is true…it doesn't work on everyone. Still, there is literally *no* therapy that works on everyone, so…meh."

A queer tone shaded Cybil's voice, a note of doubt or discomfort. Perhaps she was suspicious of hypnosis or had misgivings about her employer. Either way, the receptionist was clearly uncomfortable about something, despite her mild words.

After a while, the door opened, and a man walked out, his face red and his shoulders slumped. He approached Cybil and scheduled another appointment before leaving.

A moment later, the woman herself emerged. Dr. Poole wore her platinum hair pulled back and was dressed in a black pantsuit with a thin lapel and peplum jacket. Her collarbones protruded above the neckline of her blouse, and her head seemed to bobble precariously atop her thin shoulders.

Cybil informed her Winter was hoping to speak to her

about a personal matter. Dr. Poole turned to her. "Hello. What can I do for you, young lady?"

Winter didn't get called *young lady* very much anymore. A warm, fuzzy feeling snuggled her insides. "Hi. I'm Winter Black, a private investigator." She produced her credentials. "I need to speak with you about one of your patients who recently attempted suicide."

Dr. Poole frowned, faint lines appearing on her smooth forehead. "I'm sorry, but whatever passes between my patient and me is privileged. As I'm sure you know, I can't divulge anything discussed in therapy."

"I understand there are limitations, and it certainly isn't my intention to violate anyone's privacy. I just need to confirm a few simple facts. A client of mine, who I believe is a patient of yours…Perry Bick?"

Dr. Poole blinked a few times and crossed her birdlike arms but said nothing.

Winter pushed on. "He received a threatening letter from someone attempting to blackmail him. Has he discussed these things with you?"

The woman huffed and arched an eyebrow. Her lips remained firmly closed.

"Has Perry been undergoing hypnosis?"

She hissed out a long sigh. "I cannot discuss a patient's treatment plan."

"I understand. But would you be willing to tell me a bit more about how you generally use hypnosis as a treatment?"

Poole sniffed and rolled her neck. "If you're interested in the subject, I strongly recommend checking your local library."

Winter smiled indulgently, pushing down her urge to punch the snotty doctor right in her bleached head. "Can you confirm if another man is a patient? Robin Sheen?"

Dr. Poole rolled her eyes and sighed like she was tired of

being asked the same question. "No. I'm sorry. I wish I could be more help."

A dead dog would be more help.

"Listen, Perry already told me about what happened to him in college at EKU. He confided in me. He's hired me to help him understand what's happening to him."

She looked dubious, her eyebrows slowly rising. "I wish you nothing but luck in finding that help. But I'm sorry. When it comes to HIPAA, it's always better to err on the side of cagey."

"But your patient might be in danger."

"Many of them are and in more ways than one. That's why I'm here." She dug into her skirt pocket, took out a tiny tube, and reapplied her cherry-red lipstick.

"I'm sorry about Clarissa Toler, by the way. My condolences."

Dr. Poole visibly flinched. "I said I cannot talk about patients, Ms. Black. And I don't have time for any more of your games."

And that was exactly what Winter needed—verification that Clarissa Toler had also been a patient of Blue Tree Wellness.

"Now, if you please. I have patients to attend to." Dr. Poole pivoted on a heel and vanished behind her office door.

Winter didn't know what Dr. Poole was doing for her patients—or to them, if anything—but one was recently deceased and another was in the hospital after an attempt on his own life. After receiving Winter's fake flyers.

She gave Cybil a quick nod and exited the office, the sound of tinkling spa music fading as she left. Her suspicions were piqued, to say the least, and she intended to expose any wrongdoing before the next body dropped.

19

The man I'd traveled across town to visit was a brilliant example of the typical man that I so enjoyed working with. Like a dog, he trusted so easily. And he was so eager to please. All I had to do was throw a ball, and he'd chase it. Give him a scent of where I wanted him to go, and he would follow it halfway around the world.

I parked my car on the street and approached the bank of townhomes where Robin Sheen lived. It was late on a Tuesday night, and the street was empty. Still, I'd dressed in a black sweatshirt with the hood up, jeans, and the most basic pair of sneakers I owned. If anybody noticed me, they would register it the same way they noticed a small brown bird taking flight from a branch. The opposite of noteworthy.

Before stepping up to Robin's front door, I snapped on a pair of latex gloves. I knocked gently. Inside, he put a show on pause, and I heard his heavy footsteps loom close.

The door swung open, and the brute of a man that was Robin Sheen stood before me. He looked down and smiled, because he had affection for me. Because he trusted me.

"Oh, hi. What are you doing here?"

"Might I come in?"

"Yeah, of course." He stepped aside and held the door open. An open door made everything so much easier.

His tiny living room with the kitchen at the back smelled of curry. It was less than ideal, but you got what you got.

He closed the door and stepped up behind me. "Is everything okay?"

"Absolutely. Let's sit down, shall we?"

"Sure."

I followed him to the sofa. "I wanted to check in, and I won't be but a minute." I took a small flashlight from my pocket and shined the bright light in his eyes.

He recoiled at first, but I pressed my free hand firmly against his chest, grounding him to me. "Sleep now. Sinking down and shutting down. Sinking down and shutting down. Sinking down and shutting down, shutting down completely."

His head began to droop.

"Every word I utter is putting you faster and deeper, and faster and deeper, into a calm state of relaxation and openness. You are dropping your defenses. You are falling, faster and deeper, sinking down."

I continued to speak to him in this way, a script I'd recited so many times, I had no reason to keep my thoughts on it. Robin didn't have a convenient balcony like Clarissa, but I had other plans for him.

"It's time to go, Robin. Take the first step and feel yourself sinking deeper into relaxation. Each step is a step further into your subconscious."

Keeping him grounded with my hand, I guided him toward the side door in his town house. "With the second step, you feel yourself getting calmer and calmer. When you reach the third step, your body feels as if it is floating blissfully away."

I snatched his keys from where they hung by the door and guided him into the garage. Slowly and gently, I led him to the driver's side door of his beat-up blue 1970s Ford pickup. It was purely vintage, making the event even more poetic.

Once he was inside, I placed the keys in the ignition and started the engine. I pulled a small baggie from my pocket and dropped a single strand of hair on him.

"You know what you did, Robin. And because you do not deserve to be saved, you will stay here, and you will die."

His head lolled as he leaned back in the seat. I stayed with him a moment longer, walking him down the hypnotic staircase into a place of the deepest possible sleep. Then I closed the truck door gently and left, making certain the front door was locked and everything was sealed up tight.

I crossed through the parking lot and back to my parked car without catching sight of another soul. Within two minutes of setting Robin Sheen up in his old pickup, I was on the road.

Robin would be dead long before the break of dawn. They'd find him like that and think it was a suicide...until they slowly put the pieces together and realized the horrible truth. Or at least, the "horrible truth" I'd created for them.

I smiled at the thought of the power I held in my hands. High-maintenance Erik had actually helped unleash my powers. I'd be more grateful if he wasn't so—

My phone buzzed, derailing my train of thought. Cursing, I pulled it out and rolled my eyes. Erik, yep, again. Always Erik. He was more like a dog than any man I'd ever met, what with his puppyish need for constant attention.

I declined his call and silenced the ringer, knowing I was about to get hit by a barrage of notifications.

I wouldn't be here if not for Erik, but I'd feel more comfortable if I had some real leverage to hold over his head. All Erik really cared about was Winter Black anyway. I didn't understand his obsession, but I certainly knew how to use it against him.

20

The next morning, Winter found herself drawn back to Dr. Ava Poole's office. The woman was cagey and critical, with a poker face that many suspects in the hot seat would do well to cultivate. Winter had given up on getting anything else from her. Besides, her reaction at the mention of Clarissa Toler's name was plenty for her and Noah to work with for a while.

Still. She sensed more to learn from the wellness center.

Winter reached the lot half an hour before the doors opened, when every one of the spaces was still empty. Leaning far back in her seat, she watched a garbage truck drive in and empty a large dumpster. As the truck left, a two-door powder-blue sedan pulled in.

Out stepped Cybil, the petite, black-haired receptionist. Throwing her purse over one shoulder, she walked toward the door with a coffee mug in one hand and keys in the other.

Snatching up her own coffee, Winter exited her Pilot and jogged to catch up with Cybil. "Excuse me."

The receptionist turned and narrowed her eyes against

the light of the low-hanging sun. "I'm sorry. We're not open yet."

"That's all right. I'm sorry to bother you, but I was wondering if I could steal a minute of your time."

Her hand holding the keys slowly dropped. "You're that woman who was here yesterday." A smirk twisted one corner of her mouth, then faded into nothing. "You definitely got Dr. Poole's panties all in a twist."

Interesting.

"I'm a private investigator, and I'm working for one of Dr. Poole's patients. Would you mind if I asked you a couple of questions?"

Cybil glanced at the door and checked her watch. She shrugged and started toward a small bench in the office's front garden area among tufts of pampas grass. Winter followed, and the two women settled beside each other on the wooden slats.

Sensing that Cybil harbored at least a little animosity toward her boss, Winter decided to play that up. "I can't shake the feeling that Dr. Poole isn't being entirely honest with me."

"Can't imagine what would give you that impression." Cybil picked at the carboard sleeve on her coffee cup with the tips of her short nails.

"What do you mean?"

She sighed, her lips furling. "My mom was always a real stickler for honesty. At least when it came to me. I remember one time when I was, like, seven, I stole a candy bar. We'd already driven all the way home by the time she realized what I'd done. And the dang thing only cost maybe a buck. But she still drove me all the way back to the store and made me confess and give it back."

Winter smiled, thoughts of her own mother percolating. She didn't think about her or any aspect of her childhood very often. She tried not to look back as a rule. The good memories always spiraled into painful ones. But for one soft moment, she saw her mother's wavy black hair framing a papery-white face. Winter was tiny then, sitting in the front of the grocery cart and swinging her legs as her mom wheeled her around the store picking out apples and onions.

"That's exactly the sort of thing my mother would've done." Winter's voice cracked. She pressed her lips together to suppress a nostalgic smile and shook her head.

"Not everybody's like that." Cybil twirled a finger through her dark hair and pivoted to look directly at Winter. "You lost her."

Winter flinched and forced a laugh to help herself breathe. "Is it that obvious?"

"I'm so sorry. My mother died by suicide, so I'm sensitive to it." Cybil set her thin, pale fingers lightly on Winter's shoulder. The touch was so gentle, like a butterfly alighting on a branch. She barely felt it on a physical level, but her heart warmed, nonetheless.

"I'm so sorry for your loss."

"My dad cheated on her and left us to be with another woman who eventually tossed him out like a used tissue. It broke my mother. They both kinda killed themselves over it in the end."

Winter took a deep breath. She'd been around enough oversharers in her life—people like Cybil who seemed perfectly normal until they started belching out trauma balls. It was hard to know whether she was supposed to respond to Cybil's words or simply acknowledge their shared loss and move on. Different people wanted different reactions, and choosing incorrectly could be catastrophic for their budding rapport.

Cybil dropped her hand. She pressed her small knees tightly together, balancing the coffee cup on top with one finger on the lid. "So what do you want to know exactly? Can you tell me what you're looking for?"

"I think it's possible that somebody in the office might have used a patient's confidential information to try to exploit them."

"Oh, my goodness…" Cybil's lips parted in surprise. "I don't think so. Don't get me wrong, I don't like Dr. Poole, but she's very dedicated to what she does. She really does think she's helping her patients." She looked down at her lap. "Sometimes I wonder, though…"

"What do you mean?"

"I wonder if maybe she does what she thinks is best, whether or not the patient would agree."

"Is there anybody besides you in the office?"

"Just the cleaning lady once a week. Roberta, I think her name is…" She bit her lip and gazed off into the distance.

The sun had risen over the buildings, bathing them in a golden glow. It was going to be a hot day, and Winter could already feel the sunlight heating up the slats on the bench.

"I've only been here a few months, but there was a robbery a few weeks ago."

Winter snapped to attention. "A robbery?"

Guilt pulled at Cybil's features. "I shouldn't have told you that. Dr. Poole would be furious if she found out."

"Why?"

She looked over her shoulder as a car cruised past. It slowed for the stop sign at the corner before continuing on its way. Cybil closed her eyes, drawing her tiny, pointy shoulders up around her neck before releasing them down with a sigh. "She didn't report it."

Red flags waved wildly in Winter's brain. "Why not?"

"Because it was her fault." Cybil lifted one eyebrow, barely concealing her disdain. "She was the last one to leave the office that night, and she forgot to lock up."

"What was stolen?"

Cybil's dark eyes met Winter's. "You have to promise me not to tip off the cops."

"I'm sorry, but I can't make that promise. As a private investigator, I have certain legal and ethical obligations. If a serious crime was committed, especially one involving potential harm or injury to someone, I may be required by law to report it. I don't want to jump to conclusions, but I need to understand more about what happened before I can determine my next steps. Can you tell me more details about the situation? I want to help, but I also need to make sure I'm acting within the bounds of the law."

"But it has nothing to do with you. I don't…" Her hands tightened around her cup in frustration, denting the cardboard. One edge of the lid popped off. She fixed it quickly and set the cup on the bench beside her, running her fingers through her hair. "Will you at least keep my name out of it? I need this job. If Poole found out I snitched on her… well, Austin is smaller than you think."

"Okay." It made Winter feel a little dirty, but Cybil was shaping up to be her best source for the goings-on in Dr. Ava Poole's office. She didn't want to jeopardize that. "I can say I learned about the burglary from an anonymous tip. Can you tell me what was stolen…?"

Cybil grimaced. "When I came in that morning, the door was hanging open. I was scared, but I went inside. One of the cabinets with patient files had been pried open and rifled through. Later, when I was putting everything back in place and cross-referencing with the computer, I realized several were missing." She swallowed audibly. "One was…the woman you mentioned yesterday."

Winter drew in a long breath. "Clarissa Toler. The children's author who threw herself off a balcony."

"There was also Perry—"

"Wait. On second thought, don't tell me."

Cybil tilted her head to the side like a curious puppy. Her big black eyes only added to the effect.

"Because I'm not technically a law enforcement official. Even though I'm acting on behalf of a client, we're in a gray area regarding patient confidentiality. It would be for the best if you reported the robbery to the authorities yourself."

Cybil shook her head so hard that wisps of her black hair fell across her eyes. "Best way to get myself fired. Though I do wonder if I ought to call the patients and let them know their confidential information has been compromised. It's too late for Clarissa, but I could tell Leigh Folke—"

"Please, Cybil, don't say anything more." Winter rose from the bench.

"Dr. Poole's covering her own ass. As usual." She snarled, teeth clenching. "She doesn't care about anybody but herself. Why do people like that become doctors?"

"I don't know." That was what Winter said, but the question burrowed into her brain like an earthworm into fresh soil. According to stereotype, most people who got into mental health had problems of their own. They studied mental illness in an attempt to understand themselves.

If what Cybil said was true, and Dr. Poole genuinely didn't care about anyone other than herself, Winter could only think of one other reason why such a person would become a psychologist—to exploit a power dynamic. To stroke her own ego with the constant comparison to vulnerable people who sought her help. To manipulate them like puppets on strings.

"Thank you for your help, Cybil." Trying to conjure a friendly smile, Winter turned and walked back to her SUV.

Clarissa Toler and Perry Bick. She knew those were three of the files stolen. That was no coincidence. It wouldn't surprise her to find Robin Sheen's name on that list if she'd let Cybil continue.

But Cybil had just given her a fourth name, Leigh Folke. Exactly how many people had received an ugly flyer advertising Winter's services alongside a demand for money or death?

21

Winter drove straight to the police and asked to speak with Detective Lessner. The cop at the front desk called his office and assured Winter that Lessner would collect her soon. She settled into an uncomfortable wooden chair in a waiting area that smelled vaguely of plastic and urine.

Hey, I can smell today.

On that high note, Winter took out her phone and searched the name *Clarissa Toler*.

Books on top of books topped the search engine results. Clarissa was the author and illustrator of several dozen titles, most famously a series of chapter books called *The Fairies of Eastwind*. Winter clicked on one of them and flicked through the watercolor drawings. Then she went back and read the first few sentences on the first page.

Belinda Buttercup was the most beautiful fairy in Eastwind. The most beloved. The most kind...

Clicking on the other open tab, she scrolled down to the first article—an account of Clarissa's untimely suicide. The manner of death wasn't mentioned, though Winter knew she'd hurled herself from her balcony.

Maybe now that she had a definitive connection between Clarissa Toler, Perry Bick, and Robin Sheen, Lessner would be willing to share more information on the case. Like whether Clarissa had received a blackmail demand along with Winter's flyer.

A moment later, Lessner emerged, expression as friendly as ever. He had the sort of face that looked like it didn't know how to smile, like it was missing the muscles or something. His hangdog jowls, the deep furrow of his brow, and especially the crusty downturned lips—they all screamed, *No smiling allowed*.

When Lessner saw her, he rolled his eyes but motioned for her to follow him back.

Winter missed Darnell so much—something she thought she would never, ever admit to him. She was on the verge of calling his cell phone and bitching him out for daring to take on cases other than hers. Funny, considering how much they butted heads when they did work together.

"You don't know what you've got 'til it's gone," she heard Darnell's li'l avatar on her shoulder say.

Instead of leading her to the interview room, Lessner walked straight to his desk at a cubicle near the back of the station. She followed obediently and sat down when he gestured to a metal chair beside his desk.

Winter inspected his cubicle. Sitting on his desk was a photo of him with his arm around a woman with ginger hair and a charmingly crooked smile. His wife, she assumed.

As strange as it was to imagine him married, it was even stranger to see him smiling. Lessner looked younger in the picture, with noticeably more hair on his head. The woman wore a bikini, but Lessner had on a long-sleeved cotton shirt and pants, even at the beach. He must've been sunburned for a *last day of vacation* photo, she surmised.

"Lemme guess." He settled his dense frame into his chair. "We got another flyer?"

"Yes. A man named Robin Sheen, who's also being blackmailed by the Listener. Like me and Perry Bick and… Clarissa Toler?"

He lifted one half of his unibrow suspiciously. "Go on."

Part of Winter wanted to keep some of her information close to the vest, but she knew that would only serve to make Detective Lessner more incredulous when the truth finally came out. And she'd just cracked his poker face, so she had to keep going.

"Perry Bick attempted suicide, and he's recovering at Lakeview Hills Memorial Hospital."

Lessner sat stone-still and nonresponsive at that.

Winter played her next card in a higher suit. "I found the connection between all the blackmail targets. Her name is Dr. Ava Poole."

Lessner shifted in his seat this time. It creaked under his weight. "A doctor?"

She was reeling him in. Hopefully, he'd reciprocate in kind. "She's a psychologist who specializes in trauma treatment and hypnotherapy. Perry Bick, Clarissa Toler, and Robin Sheen are all her patients."

"Who's Robin Sheen?"

"Another target of the blackmail letter. We only just confirmed he's on the doctor's patient list too."

Lessner pulled his brows together even tighter than normal. "You suspect the doctor?"

"I did." She still did. "But I also found out that her offices were recently burglarized. And the only things that were stolen were some patient files. I'm not sure how many. Three guesses who three of them belonged to."

"Really?" At last, he sat forward, his interest transparent as a freshly squeegeed window. Lessner picked up a pencil and began scribbling notes on a yellow legal pad sitting on his desk. "Do you have the doctor's contact information?"

Winter fetched a business card from her pocket from the stash she'd taken from the doctor's office. She slid it over to Lessner.

He picked the card up, glared at it, and held it farther away from his face, like he needed reading glasses. Setting it down, he woke up his computer and tapped away at the keyboard. "Was the burglary reported?"

Winter shook her head.

His hands froze on the keys. "So how did you find out about it?"

"My source requested to remain anonymous."

"I see. Does that mean it's one of your clients with a signed confidentiality agreement in place?" Lessner was fishing, and he wasn't being subtle about it either.

Winter remained poised and folded her hands in her lap. "If you were to issue a subpoena, I'd be compelled to reveal my source. But for the moment, I don't see any benefit to the investigation in breaking my source's confidence."

He tapped the business card absently on the desktop. His eyes narrowed, as if he were deep in thought, several seconds of silence slipping away.

Winter found herself falling into the ambient noise of the station. The mumbles of officers, the beeping of phones on hold. It was all so familiar, though her memories of working in a proper law enforcement office were beginning to feel like they were from a different lifetime.

Lessner broke the silence. "Clarissa Toler was a target of the Listener."

Winter's head snapped back to attention. "I knew it."

"Like the others, it didn't specify what exactly she was being blackmailed over, but we think it's the reason she chose suicide. I've been in contact with her parents, her old friends, old boyfriends, but none of them could even guess at what dark secret she might've been hiding. There was a clue in the note, though. The secret was related to her brother."

"Have you spoken to him?"

"That's where things get a little more interesting. Clarissa didn't have a brother."

Winter nodded, unsurprised. Clarissa's blackmail note followed exactly the same M.O. as the others. A secret that was actually a lie.

Maybe Poole had committed the burglary herself as a way of trying to shift suspicion away from her. But if that were the case, why hadn't she reported it?

"Clarissa Toler was an only child. When I asked her parents about it, her mother broke into tears and told me how Clarissa had longed for a baby brother or sister when she was young, but owing to complications with Clarissa's own birth, she couldn't have any more children." Lessner tapped the eraser of his pencil. "We've been considering the possibility that *brother* is some kind of nickname."

"I doubt it."

"And why's that?"

Winter went into her laptop satchel and fetched out the evidence baggies where she'd placed the blackmail notes Perry Bick and Robin Sheen had received. She set them on the desk in front of Lessner. "When Robin Sheen received this note and one of my flyers, he was convinced I was behind everything. Once I got him to calm down, he told me an extraordinary story from his past."

She went into detail about the whole experience—how Robin's own research led him to conclude he was being blackmailed over something that never even happened.

Confusion clouded Lessner's perpetual scowl. "That doesn't make any sense."

"Not at first glance, but the more I've been over the story

with my other client, the more I found holes in his memory. It's a bit like remembering something from your childhood, only to realize it was just a dream you had."

He was glaring at her now more than ever, as if she were trying to convince him Earth was flat.

"I took a short course on hypnosis and memory during my training at Quantico. It was a long time ago, but I remember one study we had to read about. The shopping mall experiment."

He set two fingers to the side of his head and leaned back. He looked bored and incredulous before she even started.

"The experiment involved adult participants and their parents. The parents supplied researchers with stories about the participants as young children, and the researchers turned around and presented those stories to the participants. With me so far?"

Lessner grunted and shifted in his seat again.

"In addition to sharing these real stories with the participants, the researchers also shared a fake memory about the participant getting lost in a shopping mall as a young kid. It was completely made up, but do you know how many people claimed to remember the incident? Twenty-five percent."

Lessner's perpetual frown deepened. "Twenty-five percent isn't very much."

"It doesn't have to be. Dr. Poole has dozens of patients. She could have simply preyed on these particular few because they showed the greatest susceptibility to hypnosis and false memories."

"That's a pretty wild theory."

Winter shrugged, nonplussed. "That doesn't mean it isn't correct."

Lessner picked up the letter the Listener had sent to

Robin Sheen and read it over again. "Have you received any more communication?"

She shook her head.

He lowered the letter. "Thank you for bringing all this to our attention. I've applied for a warrant to get the owner information on the Paymo account provided by the blackmailer, but that'll take some time. Meanwhile, I'll check in with Dr. Poole."

Winter rose from her seat. "Please, keep me updated on any developments."

"And you the same." Over the course of their conversation, his hangdog expression had deepened while the bags under his eyes had somehow grown grayer and puffier. He looked like he wanted to lie down in a shallow hole and sleep for the next year.

Something about that—his exhaustion—gave Winter a little twist in her heart. Most LEOs ended up with some version of that look when they got on in their careers. The things they saw and dealt with over the years, the times cases went cold and justice went unserved. It grated on the soul bit by bit until it was worn down to the rind. She wondered what sad stories were hiding behind those hooded eyes.

"Be careful out there. And don't hesitate to call if you think you or any of your clients might be in immediate danger. I'd rather waste my time than see anyone get hurt."

"Thank you, Detective." She smiled softly, seeing an ally in Detective Harlan Lessner for the first time. "I hope I never need to."

22

After leaving the station, Winter called Noah and asked him to look up the fourth name Cybil mentioned—Leigh Folke.

"No problem. You got a spelling for me?" His fingers clicked on a keyboard.

"I do not. Were you able to get in touch with Robin?"

"I found a number and called it, but the voicemail was full. I'll keep looking. Okay, I'll try it with the *e* and without."

"Anything on Dr. Poole?"

Noah sighed heavily. "Nothing much. She seems to be well respected. The only black mark I could find was an ethics violation."

Curiosity stirred. "For what?"

"It was over a decade ago, but I guess she got frisky with one of her patients. Nearly had her license suspended. But it seems like she learned her lesson. Didn't find anything fishy after that."

The idea of a doctor sleeping with a patient left a bad taste in Winter's mouth, but it wasn't uncommon. And it certainly didn't lend any credence to the theory that said doctor might be an unhinged, manipulative murderer.

"Oh, here we go. Leigh Folke, F-o-l-k-e. I have her info."

"Perfect. Text it to me. Thank you."

Noah provided her with both a phone number and address for Leigh Folke, so instead of heading back to the office, Winter drove half an hour to the other side of town. She navigated through the roundabouts of the small, suburban community and found herself parking in front of a large Mexican mission-style house with pale-pink stucco on the walls and a garden filled with rocks and plump cactuses.

After texting Noah that she'd arrived, she headed up the twisting gravel path to the keyhole-shaped door, where she rang the bell and waited.

When the door opened a moment later, Winter was surprised to find herself face-to-face with the older woman she'd seen at Dr. Poole's office the day before. The one who'd been yelling at Cybil and demanding that the doctor get in contact with her as soon as possible.

She stared at Winter and planted her hands on her hips. "What?"

Leigh was wearing another velour tracksuit, this one black and trimmed with sparkles. Even with her gray hair fluffed high, she was a few inches shorter than Winter. Her fierce cheekbones pulled her skin tight. Winter wondered how many procedures the woman had undergone. Botox on her unmoving eyebrows, filler in her big fishy lips, and, of course, a good old-fashioned facelift. Up close, she looked on the other side of middle-aged.

"Hello." Winter showed a friendly smile, though her smile bank was already running precariously low so early in the day. "My name is Winter Black, P.I. I'm investigating a recent disturbance reported by some patients of Dr. Poole. Some of her patients have been receiving threatening letters. Might I ask you a few—"

"What kind of scam are you running, honey?"

Winter straightened. "I beg your pardon?"

"There are better ways to drum up business. You got a nice little figure on you. Put that on your flyer, and you'll have pervs breaking down your door to tell on themselves."

Winter took a moment to remind herself why she was there. She refused to engage in any talk of slimy pervs or flattering figures. "Let me guess…you received a flyer from my office?"

"That's why you're here, ain't it?"

"Yes, but not in the way you think."

"I'm an independent businesswoman myself. Have been for years. I know what works and what doesn't."

"Ma'am, I didn't send those flyers. They're a forgery."

Leigh raised her micro-bladed eyebrows. "Then what do you want from me? I didn't keep it. You'll have to go look at the city dump. In fact, that's exactly where I think you ought to go."

She started to close the door.

"Wait, please. I just need to ask you—"

"Time to hit the road, honey. Take a hike. Get lost."

"I need to talk to you about Dr. Poole."

She scoffed but yanked the door open again. "Unless you want to talk about what a fucking quack she is, I'm not interested."

"I'd love to know what a quack she is!"

Leigh looked her up and down and wrinkled her nose. "I seen you before. You were at the office yesterday."

"I was."

"So you're working with her. Did she hire you to come dig up dirt on me? 'Cause I'm telling you, I'm an open book. I don't give two shits."

"I believe you. But I'm not working for Dr. Poole. I'm investigating her."

That seemed to simultaneously rouse Leigh Folke's interest and lower her shields. "For what?"

"Burglary, possible HIPAA violations, maybe even worse."

A tiny smile played on the woman's lips. "Can't say I'm shocked."

"When you received my flyer, was there another note with it? A threat of blackmail maybe?"

"No. Just the flyer."

Winter was disappointed to hear that, but she didn't let it show. "Can you tell me some of the grievances you have with Dr. Poole?"

"Grievances?" She leaned against the doorframe. "Sure, I'll tell you. Dr. Poole is a moron, and her methods are a crock of shit."

Winter's smile tightened so much it stung. *Tell me how you really feel.*

"I was her patient for a year over some trauma and shit. She was recommended to me after normal talk therapy wasn't working. But Poole honestly only made things worse. Just going to her office became a trigger for me. I'd be in a panic attack before I even sat down. And then, when I left, I felt even worse. I'd get the worst headaches and dizzy spells for a couple of hours after."

"And she was hypnotizing you?"

Folke scoffed. "Supposedly."

"Did you speak to Dr. Poole about your issues? Maybe suggest altering your treatment?"

"Of course. I'm not going to pay somebody to torture me on a weekly basis and not say anything about it." She rolled her eyes. "I confronted her about it and asked her what the hell she was doing to me. And when she wouldn't answer, I threatened to sue her for malpractice."

"What did she do?"

"I can't…" She slapped her hand against the doorjamb.

"Let's just say that bitch did everything in her power to destroy and discredit me. Because of Poole and her lies, I lost my job, my husband. What little integrity I had left."

Leigh Folke's hard exterior melted just enough that Winter sensed the deep pool of suffering beneath. Whatever she'd been through had made her this way—tough and spiky on the outside. But underneath the surface was a woman in pain who'd just been looking for help and, instead, was damaged even further.

"I'm so sorry that happened to you."

In the space of a breath, Folke hardened back up. Her eyes blazed with fiery contempt. "Poole's going to get what's coming to her."

"What do you mean by that?"

She waved a dismissive hand. "It doesn't matter. And it's none of your business. Who the hell gave you my name anyway? Was it Poole?"

"No. Yours was among a group of files that was stolen from her office."

"What?" She tightened her jaw and laughed angrily. "Of course it was. Because fuck you, Leigh. Fuck you and everything you've ever been through."

A lump formed in Winter's throat as she caught a second glimpse of Leigh Folke's fiercely protected vulnerability. She swallowed it. "I think somebody might be using the information in the files to commit blackmail against the victims. Are you certain you haven't received any threatening letters?"

She shook her head. "No. And if I did, I'd burn it. Not throw myself off a balcony. I have nothing to hide."

Winter could barely conceal her shock at this statement. She was almost positive the cops had withheld information about Clarissa Toler's blackmail from the media. She herself had only found out about it earlier that morning. How the hell did Folke know about suicide-demand aspect? Not to mention, they didn't reveal the name of her therapist or any other doctors.

Maybe Leigh Folke was involved, and she'd just slipped up.

"So you and Clarissa Toler...were friends?" Winter had to fish. It was the fastest route to answers.

"Yeah, besties, we're in a book club. That reminds me, I gotta finish *Where the Crawdads Sing*. Do you mind?"

Folke's abrasive sense of humor was officially under Winter's skin. She gave her a heavy stare.

"Fine. From Poole's office. How do you think I know her? You sit there, waiting, trying not to make eye contact. But the magazines are outdated, and next thing ya know, you're talking."

"That makes sense." It did sound plausible. Whether it was true was another story.

"I didn't know her last name, but apparently she's famous, so they've been broadcasting her death like crazy, along with her photo."

Winter gave a short nod. "Thanks for your time, Leigh." After handing her business card over, she turned and headed back to her vehicle, gravel crunching under her boots. Behind her, the door slammed so loudly, it scared a flock of birds out of the Vitex tree in the front yard.

When she was safe behind the driver's seat with the doors locked, Winter took out her phone to call Noah.

It was time she learned everything there was to know about Leigh Folke.

23

Winter stepped, once again, into the spa-like waiting room of Dr. Poole's office. Enough new information had come up since yesterday afternoon that she felt compelled to interview the doctor one more time. Give Poole a chance to tell her side of the story before Winter simply assumed the worst. She was already on the verge of doing just that.

"Hey, girl." Cybil smiled and took out her earbuds. "What are you doing back so soon?"

Winter walked past the waiting area to the reception desk and leaned her elbows on the countertop. "I need to have another conversation with your boss, please."

Cybil rolled her eyes. "She's got a full roster today. And I gotta say, she is not going to be happy to see you." She looked past Winter toward a patient who was flipping through a magazine in the waiting area. "She had some choice words about you after last time you were here."

"Like what?"

"Not safe for work." Cybil leaned in as if she had a secret to tell. "She kept trying to get me to agree with her, but I just pulled a stupid face and was all, 'Really? I thought she was nice.'"

Winter smiled. "Thank you. I can use all the good PR I can get."

"I got you, girl." Cybil gave a little wink. "Anyway, Doc Poole is with a patient right now. I'm not allowed to interrupt unless, like, the building is on fire, but you can wait if you want. It shouldn't be too much longer. I'm sure she'll spot you when she steps out of her office."

"That works for me." Winter settled into one of the two bar-height chairs near the reception desk, likely intended for clients filling out quick paperwork. "I've got time."

"You want some water? We also just got some raspberry seltzer."

"That would be great, thank you."

Cybil rose from her desk, left the room, and returned with two small, fancy glass bottles, passing one over to Winter.

Unscrewing the cap, Winter sniffed the fresh raspberry bubbles, smiled at the pungent aroma, and took a sip. "You're not from Texas, are you?"

"What gave it away?"

"No accent. Whatsoever."

Cybil settled behind the desk and leaned back in her chair. "I was actually born in Austin but lived in California when I was a teenager." She played with a pen on her desk, keeping her head down.

Winter swung her legs back and forth. "I'm from Virginia myself. I only moved to Austin earlier this year."

Cybil nodded. She seemed on the verge of speaking, but every time she opened her mouth, she closed it again. Winter smiled encouragingly. Whatever Cybil knew about Dr. Poole's methods, she wanted to draw it out. For all Winter knew, Cybil was being programmed too.

After a minute of silence, Winter decided to offer up her own morsel of personal information. "I've been through some rough times myself. That's a big reason why I moved out here." She rested her elbow on the high counter and cupped her chin in her hand. "It seems like some of the things in your past also pushed you to try for a fresh start."

Cybil glanced over at the waiting area. The patient-in-waiting didn't seem to be paying attention, so she set down the pen she'd been toying with.

"My parents got a divorce when I was eleven, after my dad cheated. My mom didn't handle it well. She'd always been a really wholesome kind of lady. Never drank. Could barely bring herself to pop an aspirin. Poster child for housewifeliness. Then he left her for another woman, and suddenly she was expected to get a job on top of taking care of us."

Winter wanted to give her hug but stayed where she was. "I'm sorry."

"The pressure got to her, I guess." Her voice transformed from friendly and welcoming to cold and spiky. "She got so depressed and was having all kinds of trouble sleeping. So the doctors gave her meds for it."

Oh, no. Winter had a feeling she knew where this story was going.

Cybil picked up her drink and took a sip as if the story was over, though her dark eyes said otherwise. After another sip, she added, "And one night, she took a whole bottle and never woke up."

Winter's heart cracked like concrete left in the cold. She pressed a hand to her chest to try to hold back the pain. "I'm so sorry."

Cybil's story sure felt authentic and unprogrammed. But still, the tale sounded just wild and dramatic enough to be a false memory.

"I went to live with my dad, but he was useless after he'd been dumped by the woman he'd left us for. Here I was having just lost my mother, and he was out getting drunk every night." Cybil's eye glossed with tears waiting to spill. "One night, he didn't come home at all, and I found out he'd wrapped his car around a tree. He died in the hospital a few days later."

Wilder and wilder.

Cybil aggressively wiped the heel of her hand over both eyes. "I have no idea why the hell I just told you that. I'm sorry." She looked over at the slumped patient in the waiting area and whisper-shouted, "Sorry."

They looked up as if their name had been called for their appointment. On realizing it wasn't, they settled back into a dull stare.

"No, it's okay." Winter pressed her lips together tight. Part of her wanted to open up, too, but she didn't want to get into a contest over who had the worst childhood. Besides, it seemed rude. And there was an audience, however inattentive they might've been. Cybil came across as a nice girl, if a little twisted. Winter didn't want to seem like she was downplaying what she'd gone through.

"I kind of want to give you a hug," Winter admitted.

Cybil laughed in her throat, a choked and painful little noise. She didn't say no, so Winter walked behind the desk. She wrapped her arms around Cybil's shoulders and squeezed. Cybil tensed at first but then relaxed, resting her head on Winter's shoulder.

"You've been through it too," Cybil whispered.

Winter pulled back. It wasn't a question, but a statement. "You know who I am, don't you? I mean, my background."

Cybil's eyes popped open—sparkly and innocent like a child's, gazing unashamedly into Winter's eyes. "When we first met, I thought your name sounded familiar. I googled you." She looked down, her cheeks reddening. "I'm sorry. I mean, about what happened to you. To your family."

Winter swallowed the lump in her throat. She'd never get used to her celebrity—the fact that anybody who heard her name could so easily associate her with her infamous little brother, whose name fit neatly into a list of the most recognizable serial killers in American history. Ted Bundy, John Wayne Gacy, Richard Ramirez. Justin Black.

"Thank you." Winter licked her lips and forced a smile.

When she thought about Justin and Douglas Kilroy—the man who killed her family and molded her brother into the monster he became—one of two things usually happened. Either Winter traveled through memories and flashbacks, like Alice walking through a nightmarish Wonderland, or she'd dissociate and get lost entirely. And she didn't want to do either. She wanted to stay in the moment and in control.

"Is it true your brother tried to get you to join him?" Cybil asked in a scratchy whisper. "Were you ever tempted?"

Winter shuddered, a painful tremor rushing down her spine. She was about to respond when the door to Dr. Poole's office cracked open. Winter flinched and hopped back, her fight-or-flight mode fully activated.

A woman with red streaks on her cheeks and a tissue clenched in her hand stepped out. Glancing at Cybil and Winter, she nodded politely and rushed out of the office.

A moment later, Dr. Poole called out through the door. "Cybil, tell my two o'clock I'm running a little late. I have to get some food in me, or I'm going to…" She peeked her head out of the office, saw Winter, and immediately tensed like a dog finding a stranger in its house. "…die."

"Good afternoon, Dr. Poole." Winter smiled politely. "Could I trouble you for another moment of your time?"

The doctor glared at her receptionist and stiffened her neck. "You have five minutes."

With that, she turned like a tin soldier and marched back into her office. Winter's gaze lingered on Cybil a moment longer before she followed the pissed-off doctor.

24

Sitting at the small reception desk in Winter's office, Noah must've watched twenty clips of news coverage on Clarissa Toler's death and read at least as many articles. Most of them were very bare bones on the details, summarizing date, time, and place, before shifting tone to talk about Toler's life and the legacy she left behind.

Many of them included resources for anybody who might be considering ending their lives. One of the more recent articles mentioned that her parents had set up a charity in her name to help pre-teens and other youth who might be struggling with suicidal thoughts.

Nowhere was a blackmail letter mentioned. Nowhere did the name Dr. Poole come up, or even the fact that Clarissa Toler had been seeing a therapist.

Perhaps Leigh Folke recognized Clarissa from a book signing or author event. Or perhaps the two women really did meet in the waiting room of Blue Tree Wellness center. Noah wasn't ruling anything out, even the theory that Folke was the one who sent the letter.

With that in mind, he moved on to the next assignment Winter had given him—Leigh Folke's background.

As usual, he started his research by simply googling the name. Though he'd already used his reverse lookup software to get Folke's address and number, he still found that a simple internet search could at times provide the best results.

The name Leigh Tabitha Folke populated on his screen, along with an image of a woman in her mid-sixties with a mop of silver curls and cheekbones that could cut glass. Below that was a short list of articles about local artist Leigh T. Folke. She was an artist, and Toler was an author, strengthening the odds that their paths could've crossed at any number of local art festivals too.

He clicked on the first link—an announcement in the local paper of the opening of an art show.

Prepare to be enchanted at the upcoming interactive art exhibit, "Mirror Magic," by the visionary artist Leigh T. Folke. This immersive experience blurs the lines between reality and fantasy, guiding viewers into a world where art and magic interlace seamlessly.

Another article farther down took a similar tone.

Folke's masterful creations transport you through mesmerizing visual storytelling. Interactive installations invite you to participate, offering a deep connection to the magical realm she crafts.

Noah dug a little farther and found a biographical write-up on her on the community page for a public library, where she'd hosted a free, four-week workshop on interactive art for elementary children. A group photo showed a bunch of kids falling over themselves to get closer to her. All smiles and hugs and wild hair. Everyone, including Folke, looked genuinely happy.

After reading the bio word for word, Noah dashed out a summary to send to Winter. Leigh Folke wasn't always an artist. The daughter of Hungarian immigrants, she grew up in New York City and left home at sixteen. She spent the next few decades as a vagabond, bouncing between Europe, the U.S., and South America.

In her travels, Folke dabbled in pretty much every creative occupation—actress, spoken word poet, caricaturist, street performer, pony trainer in Italy, tour guide in the north of Scotland. Just before settling in Austin, she'd worked as a performer on the Vegas Strip.

The article didn't say what kind of performer. In Las Vegas, she could have been anything from a stand-up comedian to a trapeze artist to a burlesque singer. He glanced back at the name of her most recent show, "Mirror Magic," and couldn't help but wonder…

Hypnotism acts used to be all the rage in Las Vegas. Winter had theorized that Robin Sheen and Perry Bick had been implanted with false memories via hypnotism. Perhaps it was possible their perpetrator was a stage magician instead of a trained therapist.

He shot off an email of his early findings to Winter before doing a deep dive into Folke's time in Vegas. She'd moved to Austin nearly ten years ago, so it was going to take some digging.

Before he dove in, Noah went into the break room and poured himself another cup of coffee. He hoped Ariel would come back soon. He felt a bit silly trapped in the office while Winter was out there all on her own. The whole point of his sabbatical from the FBI was so he could be at her side, protecting her. Partners in anti-crime, just like they used to be.

He tapped his fingers against his mug. At least he was available to back her up at any moment, but he needed to let her be the one to ask for him, not the other way around. Winter had always been hard to hold on to. The sort of woman who felt suffocated by anyone clinging too closely. He needed to show her that he'd be there to help at her discretion, and someday soon—he hoped—she'd ask him to work at her side.

He sighed and returned to Ariel's—his for now—desk. He just needed to be patient.

25

As Winter followed the doctor into her office, she noted that Dr. Poole's admirable calm from twenty-four hours ago was fraying. Her hair was done up in a braid twisted around her head, but it was frizzy, a classic *I didn't wash my hair and I don't want anyone to notice* kind of style. As she sat down behind her desk, she wrung her hands together, crossing and uncrossing her legs.

"Are you doing all right, Doctor?" Winter's tone was smooth and friendly. She worked to keep her face blank, though she couldn't help feeling a little uncomfortable in Dr. Poole's presence.

If her suspicions about the doctor were true, then this was a woman who possessed an almost supernatural ability to influence the minds of others.

Winter hoped she wouldn't be susceptible to such a thing, but overconfidence was always the enemy of caution. "If you're hungry, please, eat your lunch. I understand I'm interfering with your workday."

"I'm fine." Dr. Poole pulled back her shoulders and

straightened her neck. Poised and professional. "I imagine you'll be delighted to hear that I, too, have received a letter."

Winter was hardly delighted, but she was instantly captivated. "Was it signed?"

Dr. Poole's eyes narrowed into slits. Exhaling a defeated, painful sigh, she dropped her forehead into her hand. "Yes, the Listener."

"Did you receive it at your home or here at the office?"

"The office. Cybil brought it in with the mail yesterday, though there wasn't a stamp on it."

Winter slid into the chair across from the doctor. "That fits with all the others. They were hand delivered. Might I see it?"

The woman shook her head so frantically, Winter worried she might sprain her neck. "Absolutely not."

Taken aback, Winter folded her hands in her lap. The timing of Dr. Poole's letter was rather convenient. She was a very intelligent woman. If she were the one behind all this, she knew full well she'd be at the top of a list of suspects. Casting herself as another victim seemed the obvious strategy to divert suspicion away from her own person.

But if that were the case, she should've been anxious to produce the letter.

"Please. Any single piece of evidence could be the key to catching the Listener and putting an end to all this. I understand if you won't share it with me, but you need to give it to the police. It's the right thing to do. For yourself and your patients."

"I said no." Cracks formed at the edge of the doctor's voice.

Winter was confused. Robin Sheen, Perry Bick, and Clarissa Toler's letters had all been stingy with the details about what exactly they were being blackmailed over. If the doctor's was the same—and logic dictated it would be—she had no reason to be cagey about it.

Maybe they weren't the same.

"Was your letter typewritten?"

She nodded, her gaze pointed out the window at a few little sparrows hopping about on a nearby branch.

"What did they ask for?"

"That's the strange thing. They didn't ask for anything. They just…" Dr. Poole tightened her white cardigan around her shoulders. It wasn't at all cold in her office, but she certainly looked chilled. Her bones seemed fragile, avian. The sunlight on her face and on her hands illuminated every crepe-like wrinkle.

The fear in her eyes looked as real as any Winter had ever seen. A deep, primal dread that kept her head on a swivel and robbed her of sleep. She looked like somebody who knew she was being watched.

Granted, Dr. Poole might've simply been an excellent actor. Given her intimate understanding of human behavior, Winter would hardly be surprised.

"They just threatened me with some nonsense from my past." The doctor's lips hardened, whitening from the pressure. "What do you want anyway?"

Note to self. Have Noah do a very deep dive into Dr. Ava Poole.

"I have a few more questions. About Perry Bick." Winter didn't want to jump straight into an interrogation. She didn't have any evidence on the doctor yet, and that was always easier to collect when the suspect didn't yet know they were under suspicion.

Dr. Poole's lips thinned further, if that were even possible. "I told you. I cannot disclose patient details. If that's all y—"

With a rustle, Winter produced a signed HIPAA release form from her satchel. On the way over, she'd swung by the hospital to get the signature from Perry.

It didn't take long for Dr. Poole to scrutinize the document and lay it aside on her desk. She sighed. "All right, then. Go on."

"In interviewing Perry Bick, I've found some of the details of his story don't match up."

Dr. Poole nodded without hesitation. "Yes, I noticed that when you were here yesterday."

"What do you mean?"

"Perry Bick attended college at Vanderbilt University in Nashville. I remember that vividly, because I did a presentation there a while back. And when Perry found out, we had a long conversation about the school. But when you were here, you seemed rather confident he'd been in school in Kentucky."

Winter nodded as well, both impressed and encouraged. Her HIPAA release form covered only so much disclosure of medical information, but she decided to push a little further. "He actually attended EKU for his first semester."

"Oh, yes, that's right. But he's a Commodore through and through."

"But I think the story he told me, everything, was a lie. I also think he fully believes it."

The doctor rolled her neck, pressing her fingertips into the muscles. She was clearly weighing how much to share. "Perry's a very suggestible individual. He's suffered some traumatic experiences that have left him often seeking refuge from his own memories. But until last month, he'd never had any problems distinguishing fantasy from reality."

"You've noticed a recent change in him?"

"Oh, yes." Dr. Poole steepled her long fingers. "Details of old stories have been changing. He's been saying things I know to be untrue. Trivial details, mostly. Dates, places. Nothing major, simply details that don't correspond with my notes."

So an outside party, possibly the thief who stole the patient files, was altering Perry Bick's memories. Or Dr. Poole was trying to steer Winter away from the notion that she, an expert in hypnosis, was doing it. Both options left Winter asking why. Assuming the psychologist was an evil mastermind, altering her patients' memories and convincing them to end their lives by suicide—why? What did she have to gain?

Doctors often did decades' worth of research for case studies. Was this part of some breakthrough trial Dr. Poole wanted recognition for? Or was it less complicated than that? Did she simply enjoy pushing people to the brink?

Winter could hardly ask her outright, so she went another way. "Do you have any idea why a patient might do such a thing? Why their memories might change?"

"There are a few possible explana…" She pressed her lips together. "I've already said too much."

Winter forced back her irritation and impatience. She didn't want to give Dr. Poole an opportunity to shut down, so she changed the subject. "What do you plan to do about the letter?"

"What is there to do?"

"Hand it over to the police and let them do their job."

Dr. Poole bristled and looked at the small but ornate gold watch on her thin wrist. "I have another appointment. If there isn't anything else…"

"I understand you had a burglary in the office recently. Is that true?"

Her eyes widened. A little wrinkle the shape of a bolt of lightning creased the space between her eyes.

"You really ought to report that, or you might find yourself involved in several lawsuits. Patients don't appreciate when their private information is leaked. Neither does the U.S. government."

"I have no idea what you're talking about." Dr. Poole placed both her palms on the desk and pushed herself to stand. "I'd like you leave now."

"Sure." Winter rose and exited the office, shutting the door behind her. Stepping into the reception area, she noticed a man sitting in one of the bar-height chairs at Cybil's desk, filling out paperwork. A new patient, no doubt.

Cybil motioned for Dr. Poole's next patient to go on back.

Crossing the reception area, Winter found her gaze drawn to a faint, pale-red glow on top of the pile of magazines. She stopped short.

As a child, Winter had suffered brain damage at the hands of the man who murdered her parents and tortured her little brother, an event that gifted her with a sixth sense. Sometimes, she'd have visions of the past or the future. Sometimes, her dreams contained symbols pointing to truths she could not otherwise know.

And sometimes, she would simply see a strange red glow around a particular object that always helped lead her to the truth.

She glanced over one shoulder. Cybil was distracted by the new patient, who seemed to be having some trouble answering the questions on the form. She was giving him step-by-step instructions.

Winter approached the square coffee table in the center of the waiting area.

The glow was coming from a local Austin freebie. As her fingers touched the circular, the glow started to fade.

"Cybil?" Winter lifted the paper in the air. "Do you mind if I take this?"

"What?" She sounded a little frazzled. "Oh, um. Is it from today?"

She glanced at the date. "Nearly two weeks old."

"Be my guest. I just recycle them anyway."

"Thank you." Stuffing the paper under her arm, Winter left the office. She made a beeline from the front door to her Pilot, only pausing when she was in the driver's seat with the doors locked and the ignition started.

Her pulse quickened as she unfolded the paper. When she got to the central pages, she gasped. Several letters had been cut out. She would wager significant money that the missing letters formed the blackmail letter sent to her office.

Her desire to get the hell away from Dr. Poole's office redoubled. Winter folded the paper back up, dropped it on the passenger seat, clicked her seat belt, and pulled out of the lot.

She wondered why such damning evidence had been left out in the open for her to find. One logical conclusion was that the Listener wanted her to.

Finding the paper at Dr. Poole's office strengthened Winter's suspicions of the doctor in one sense and weakened them in another. Dr. Poole seemed like a reasonable and intelligent woman. If she committed a crime, particularly inciting murder, she was smart enough to do everything she could to get away with it. She wouldn't leave damning evidence out in her waiting room. Not unless this was part of her scheme to shift the blame onto someone else in the office.

If somebody was framing Dr. Poole, they'd left the circular in exactly the right spot. That could be the whole point of this scheme. Somebody with an axe to grind was going out of their way to destroy the doctor's life. Framing her for murder would be a great way to do that.

Still, Winter couldn't put her own threatening letter out of her mind. The Listener was doing this for her sake too. Distributing false flyers and making threats relating to her aunt, who virtually no one knew about.

The problem was, Winter couldn't see any logical

connection between herself, Dr. Poole, and all her other patients. What person could possibly be looking to harm them both—or all of them—in equal measure? Unless Dr. Poole was simply clever enough to make it seem like she was being framed. The office burglary, Winter receiving her own letter, Dr. Poole receiving a blackmail letter…it could all be a front to deflect suspicion.

And Leigh Folke had not escaped Winter's suspicion either. Of all the patients who had their files stolen, she alone had not received a threatening letter—or so she claimed.

Winter took out her phone to call Noah for updates on Leigh Folke when she noticed he'd already sent her an email on the subject.

He was turning out to be a damn fine assistant. She had to give him that.

26

Back at the police station in the interview room with the eternally exasperated Detective Lessner, Winter showed him the newspaper she'd found at Dr. Poole's office. She was spending so much time at the station for this case, she was starting to feel less like a P.I. and more like a contractor or consultant. Was she actually getting paid for any of this?

Perry Bick had signed on as her client, but she'd forgotten to collect a retainer. She'd gotten so used to Ariel handling all those little details, like money and binding contracts, that it had slipped her mind, and now he was in the hospital, out of commission.

Winter sighed thinking of it, her spirits dropping. She missed Ariel.

Lessner had his lunch spread out on the table—a crispy chicken sandwich and pile of waffle-cut fries with viscous pink sauce on the side and a soda the size of a milk carton. He chewed in one cheek as he glanced over the paper, which Winter had since placed into an evidence baggie.

He burped quietly into his elbow before picking up his soda. "You took this from her office?"

"With permission. It was about to be thrown in the trash."

He tilted his head and swallowed audibly. "Weird she'd just leave it out."

That was an excellent point, one that had been circling around Winter's head ever since she saw the red glow. "Can you match the cutouts to those in the letter I was sent?"

"I'll add it to the other evidence for processing. I'm afraid I don't have any good news on that front. Whoever wrote the letters was gloved up. The only partial prints we've been able to lift belonged to the victims."

Winter set a hand on the back of the chair next to her and leaned back. Her stomach was grumbling at the smell of the fries, but she didn't want to eat. Every organ in her body vibrated on high alert, the blood forced into her limbs, gearing her up to either fight a tiger or run screaming at a moment's notice. "Victims? As in plural?"

Lessner sucked on his plastic straw. "Have you heard about Robin Sheen?"

Oh, no. "What about him?"

"Just more bad news, I'm afraid. His body was discovered in his garage this morning."

Dammit.

With her thoughts consumed by Perry and his attempted suicide, Leigh Folke, and Dr. Poole's possible involvement, Robin Sheen had slipped off her radar. Plus, he'd come off as stronger than Perry, more in control of the situation. Winter had naively thought the man was impervious to implanted suggestions because he knew his memories were false. "How? Who found him?"

"He had plans with some friends to go golfing this morning. One came by to pick him up. He knocked on the door. No answer. So he went to the garage door and knocked there. When there was no answer again, he peeked through the window and found Sheen slumped in the driver's seat of his truck."

"Death by suicide?" Now she knew for sure Clarissa Toler's death was not a suicide any more than Robin Sheen's was.

Lessner nodded, the skin on his neck folding. "That's how it seems. The friend called 911, but he was pronounced dead at the scene. Had been hours by then. Carbon monoxide poisoning."

"No." Winter shook her head. "No, I don't buy it."

"I had a feeling you might say that."

"He had no reason. Robin Sheen had resolved not to let the blackmailer have any power over him." Winter rubbed her temples. "He already confessed to the crime he assumed they were talking about and found out there were glitches in his memory. That he wasn't even guilty of anything. He said he didn't even care if the story got out. Said it wasn't worth thirty grand to hide it."

"No signs of a struggle at the scene. No wounds on the body. No forced entry."

"Just like Clarissa Toler, right?" Winter raked her fingers through her hair. This had to be one of the most frustrating cases she'd ever dealt with. The only evidence she ever seemed to get was a lack of evidence. Or more glib communication from the enigmatic *Listener*.

"I agree with you that something very strange is happening, but I'm not sure if I buy the idea that somebody can hypnotize somebody else into killing themselves. You have to admit it's far-fetched."

She dropped her hands into her lap. "Just because something seems strange doesn't mean it isn't happening. I'm not floating silly magical theories here. Hypnotism and the power of suggestion are documented phenomena."

"Granted. I didn't say it was impossible. It's just that I

associate coerced suicide with group settings involving ritual and systemic brainwashing, like with Heaven's Gate."

"No. This isn't like that at all. In a cult, people are indoctrinated into a belief system, not hypnotized. Hypnotism is about accessing the subconscious, bypassing the part of the brain that needs to be convinced with logic. The same part of the brain that would be able to stomp on the brakes. My working theory is that these particular victims were chosen based on their susceptibility to hypnosis."

She drummed her nails on the arm of her chair, the soft clicks forming an even softer echo in the corners of the room. "The Listener is smart. They know what they're doing. They are expertly staging murders to look like suicides. And, in addition to finding victims who are easily hypnotized, they're selecting people with histories of mental problems, so it's easier for others to accept the victims did this to themselves."

"I really shouldn't tell you this," Lessner cut in, "but there is some evidence that Robin Sheen wasn't alone when he got into the truck that night."

Her skin prickled like she'd hopped into a hot tub after rolling naked in the snow. "Really? What?"

"I'm not at liberty to disclose the details."

He literally was at liberty, just choosing not to tell her.

"But," Lessner continued, "we have physical evidence that Sheen was somewhere around a Caucasian female within hours of his death."

Caucasian female. Dr. Poole and Leigh Folke both fit that description. No reason not to throw Cybil Kerie onto that list. Anyone with access to files or patients at the Blue Tree Wellness Center was suspect.

"I'm only trying to help," Winter reminded him.

"I know. But if you decide to go all vigilante again, it'll be my ass in the hot seat. And I don't like to have a hot ass. Not at all."

God, she missed Darnell. He never seemed to give shit either way. As much as he complained about the trouble she got him into, he never hesitated to dive back in headfirst. Lessner, on the other hand, was so afraid of trouble that he didn't even want to discuss the possibility of breaking any rules.

Winter stifled a painful groan. "When you get anything more, please, call me."

She knew he already had her number, but she left him her business card just in case he needed a reminder. Then she left the interview room without another word.

27

After a dinner of Cajun shrimp carbonara lovingly prepared by her budding chef of a husband, Winter and Noah settled down on the porch with a bottle of wine. They were facing the wrong direction to properly watch the sunset—though the sunrise from the front porch was gorgeous—but the sky with its pale pinks and orange-dusted clouds was still a worthy sight.

Winter rested her back against Noah's chest, her feet up on the swing as he gently rocked the two of them back and forth on his heels and ran his fingers through her hair. Her eyelids drooped, even as her brain continued buzzing. She was thinking about Opal, about Kline. Wishing one was still alive, wondering if that would've kept the other from leaving.

All her life, Winter had carried a vague jealousy, even resentment, of people who were lucky enough to grow up with families. Even broken and dysfunctional ones. That feeling had abated somewhat when she met Autumn—her best friend and former colleague—and later Noah, the love of her life. But tonight, that old pit in her stomach was back.

She hadn't fully admitted it yet, but part of her thought

Kline would be an opportunity to start over. To finally have a father she could turn to. Someone to rely on. Someone to teach her what things had been like before she was born.

Now that he was gone—of his own free will—she kind of wished she'd never known about him at all. Better to just have a dead father than to find out the man she thought was her father wasn't, that her "real" biological father was just… well, a massive disappointment.

Winter physically choked on the thought and cleared her throat. It felt cruel to think that about him, but she couldn't help it. Kline had said he wanted to make up for lost time. Instead, he'd done a little bit of handy work, which she'd paid him for, and then vanished like a thief. Like a no-account vagabond.

And that was exactly what he was. He stole a dead man's name and used it to hide from all semblance of responsibility. From reality. And now she was just another thing for him to hide from. If he bolted because they wanted him to turn himself in for identity fraud…it seemed like such a small crime in the grand scheme. Not enough to be a tipping point.

"Where are you, darlin'?" Noah's gentle fingers brushed her cheek, and she looked up at him. A soft smile immediately broke across her face. The man she chose to love couldn't have been more different from her father. He was her family, and she trusted him implicitly. She knew he'd never leave, no matter what.

Winter snuggled deeper into him, sighing as his arms tightened around her shoulders. It was the best place to feel safe, and safety was so hard to find.

"Nowhere that I want to be thinking about."

He didn't press the issue. "I spoke to the police chief down at the station. He says Davenport won't be back for another two weeks or more. A suspect in a string of old homicides is standing trial for crimes in New Mexico. Davenport is helping the prosecution with the criminal profile, and then he'll be extraditing him back to Texas to stand for the crimes he committed here."

Winter pressed her hands into his chest, lifting her head to gaze into his eyes. "I don't remember asking you to do that."

"I ain't your minion. I think you'll find I do all sorts of things you don't ask me to do."

She laughed and relaxed back against him. "You're a terrible assistant. It's a miracle you filed any comprehensible reports at the Bureau. You're all typos and dropped articles. Like I can even read your shorthand."

"Are you saying you can't?"

She could, but still.

"You mentioned this new guy is getting on your nerves."

"Way to change the subject. Lessner?" Winter rolled her eyes and sipped her wine. "He's fine. Just a bit…I don't know. Crotchety, I guess."

"A cop that's crotchety? Imagine that."

Winter laughed, then sobered as a picture of Lessner came into her mind. "He's just one of those people who wears his face like a mask and never seems to get excited about anything. It's frustrating. He makes me feel like I'm being unreasonable."

"There's nothing wrong with having passion for what you do. It's one of the things I love about you."

"Right back at you, baby." She took his hand in hers and kissed his knuckle.

"I started reading a book about stage magic."

"Really?"

"It's kinda old, from the eighties, I think. But the forums online suggested it's a classic."

"What's it called?"

"The Enchanted Trance: Mastering the Art of Mesmerism."

"You know, when you said you were gonna make money while you were off work, I had no idea you were planning to completely change careers." She poked him in the ribs. "Are we gonna have to move to Vegas?"

He ignored her, like he often did when she was being a pain in the butt, which usually only encouraged her. But Winter closed her mouth this time.

"It says the most important aspect of group hypnotism is the correct selection of subjects. The author is really plainspoken about the process. Like, he's not trying to maintain the mystery at all. He straight-up says that social pressure is a big part of what makes the trick work."

"Social pressure?"

"The expectation of the audience for the hypnotized person to perform." Noah made slow, lazy circles with his fingers on her upper arm, sending tingles across her skin. "Most people can't resist the social pressure. They don't want to be the reason the show stalls. So even though they aren't hypnotized at all, they'll go ahead and cluck like a chicken when they're told to because that's what is expected of them. It's the magician's job to screen out the noncompliant ones. That's the real trick."

Winter ran her finger lightly along the rim of her crystal glass until a faint note trilled. "So that could have a lot to do with the seemingly random selection of victims. What they have in common is compliance."

Noah nodded thoughtfully. "He also has an entire chapter about the power of authority. I was surprised, but he talks about several examples of people acting against their own morals and upbringing and beliefs, all for the sake of pleasing an authority figure. Everything from Nazi Germany to the Stanford Prison Experiment."

"Interesting."

Reaching for the wine bottle, Noah topped off both their glasses. "In order to be a successful *mesmerizer*...that's the term he prefers, not *hypnotist*...a magician first has to display total control over the audience and environment. That's why, he says, he never opens with mesmerism. You have to prove you're a confident and capable magician first or nobody will fall for it."

Winter sat up straight, his words bubbling through her like a quick jolt of caffeine. "That would be another strike against Dr. Poole. She's definitely in a position of authority."

"Maybe. Or it could be anybody who understands the principles. Leigh Folke, for example." Noah sipped his wine.

"I thought you couldn't confirm she did magic."

Noah had given Winter a rundown on what he'd found on the bohemian artist over dinner. The fact that her art exhibit in Austin contained the word *magic* had set off alarm bells, but that word could mean so many things.

"No, I couldn't. I looked through archives of Vegas shows, but no luck. I don't even know what casino she was at or for how long. Still, it's not an unreasonable assumption."

"You know what they say about assumptions."

"I'm just going off your hypnotism theory. It doesn't seem like a skill that takes a PhD to learn. All it takes is confidence and understanding of how the human mind works." Noah eased back onto the swing, and Winter leaned into him again. "The social and mental pressures that will cause people to perform. If whoever did this also had access to their psychological profiles, they'd have a skeleton key into their psyche."

Winter nodded. "I know Leigh Folke and Perry Bick have both been treated for PTSD. I wonder if there's a way someone could manipulate a person's triggers to implant memories or make them do things. When you're in a triggered state or having a flashback, the reasonable part of your brain kind of goes on vacation."

"Yep." He tightened his arm around her, protective and gentle and strong all at once. Everything she needed him to be. He knew exactly what she was talking about, as he suffered from the same condition.

As an OEF combat veteran, Noah could've given a dissertation on the subject. He had his own triggers. Fireworks, barking dogs, the squeal of brakes. Very crowded places, especially if it was indoors. Anywhere he felt like he couldn't make a quick exit. Sometimes, just the sight of soldiers in uniform was enough. Or an old woman in a hijab, especially if she was upset.

His worst trigger was children screaming. Even if they weren't in any trouble and were simply screaming for fun, like kids did. Noah's body would tense up, his eyes would go dark, and Winter would know he wasn't with her anymore.

"I read another article that says it's actually very possible to implant false memories without hypnotism." The swing moved back and forth, back and forth, in a lulling rhythm. "It's just a manipulation technique. Stems from the same kind of selective problems you have with victim and eyewitness testimony sometimes. People can be convinced they saw things they didn't. Details they know aren't real or that lawyers made up just to test them. I'm sure you've seen it happen a thousand times, just like me."

"That's a really good point." Winter sat up and pulled her knees tight against her chest. "So it's possible we're not looking for a hypnotist at all, maybe not even a therapist. Just somebody who's good at setting themselves up as an authority and manipulating people."

Noah sighed. "I know that makes this more complicated."

"No, you're right. Tunnel vision is never a good thing." Winter set her chin on her knees. "I think I need to have another conversation with Leigh Folke. The fact that she's the only one whose file was stolen and who has allegedly received no demands for money is suspicious. I'll see if I can get anything more out of her then."

"I found the number of a guy who called himself a Las Vegas historian. I'm gonna give him a call in the morning and see if he can help me track down Folke's past." Gently, he drew her back down to him.

"Perfect. Not to mention, since Robin Sheen's death, if Folke isn't responsible, she could be next on the Listener's list. With or without a blackmail note." Winter bumped her shoulder against Noah's. "All right, admit it."

"Admit what?" He screwed up his face in confusion.

"You are my good minion."

28

I had only just decided what to watch on TV while I ate my dinner of leftover pizza when my phone started ringing. I'd given Erik his own special ringtone, "Shut Up and Let Me Go" by The Ting Tings. It encapsulated exactly how I felt every time I was forced to talk to him. But on the flip side, I liked the song. So I could at least get some pleasure from his inevitable interruptions.

I wanted to ignore him, but I'd ignored his last six calls. As much as I was loath to admit it, we were still in this together.

Sighing, I set aside my plate and picked up the phone. "Hello?"

"About damn time!"

I pulled the phone away from my ear at his screeching. "What do you want?" I was already bored by the conversation.

"You've got your target practically tearing her hair out, but what about mine? You told me you'd hypnotize her."

I had to laugh at that. I actually wished he was standing right in front of me so I could laugh right in his stupid face.

"It's not magic, you idiot. These things take time. It took a couple of months to get the others to the place I wanted them, and Winter Black's much more suspicious than any of them. What exactly do you expect from me?"

"I expect for you to hold up your side of the damn bargain." His sneer rang through the line. "I expect you to churn up drama and help me drive that bitch out of her mind. You wouldn't be anywhere without me. I expect you to know your place and pull your—"

"Yes, I get it. I wouldn't have been able to talk Toler or Sheen into taking their lives without you. And Bick? I'll circle back or figure it out if I need to." I sighed heavily. "And I've already helped you with Winter. She's all over the office. I promise she's pulling her hair out, too, just not in the same way. But I can't force my way inside her mind. She's not vulnerable like the others. Probably because she's been mind-fucked so hard in the past, she's built up some resilience. What do you want with her anyway?"

"That's my business. You just need to play your role."

"Or what, Erik?" It sounded like there was an ultimatum at the end of his sentence, and I didn't like it one bit.

"Or you know what."

"If you turn me into the police for Toler and Sheen, then how do you plan on getting closer to Winter? Your other lackeys have failed at every turn. She's outsmarted all of them, according to you. Who needs who now?"

"Fine. Fine! But don't you forget who's in charge here. Remember which one of us has the resources to make this work."

The man did have money and connections both on the dark web and in the real world.

"Listen, you have to be patient. Think of me like a vampire, not a magician. I have to be invited in."

"I don't need your stupid metaphors. I need results."

I looked at my pizza and my TV. My pleasant evening had slipped away. "She found the newspaper you asked me to plant in the office."

"She did? What did she do?"

"She asked if she could take it with her."

"Okay, cool."

Unable to resist, I took a bite of my pizza. "What the hell was that for anyway?"

"I sent her a personal letter. I went old school. Cut out the words from that paper. I wanted to make sure she knows this case is personal."

"Did you say it was from the Listener?"

"Of course. How else would she know?"

My hand clenched into a fist. "You stupid fuck! Why would you do that?"

"I told you why. I need results. I need to see Winter cracking. I need her to know the walls are closing in."

"But I'm the Listener. Not you! And now you've connected yourself to the office. To me! And connected Winter Black to me directly! This could ruin everything for me." I punched the couch, mentally kicking myself for setting that paper out for her to find. Why had I trusted him? If I wasn't careful, Erik's recklessness and my compliance were going to lead that observant P.I. right to my doorstep. Shit, she'd already rung the proverbial doorbell and invited herself in for coffee.

"It doesn't matter," Erik insisted, not sounding the least bit intimidated by my outburst. "I was just trying to liven things about a bit. Light a fire under her ass."

"That's all we need. A fire under Winter Black's ass. She's already following our every footstep. Do you know what she's capable of?"

"I know who she is!"

His shriek pierced my ear like a toothpick. After that, I

couldn't fully understand what he said. He was spitting and hissing and barely able to form words.

"Calm down, Erik. Seriously, you're acting like a toddler. I want to get away with this. I want us both to get a chance to finish what we started." I flexed my fingers, trying to release the tension vibrating through my body. "But you can't roll me into your Winter Black vendetta. I just agreed to be the messenger, to throw the police off your tail, to pave the way for you to kill her or do whatever the hell."

Erik was a petulant child, but one who knew my darkest secrets. Spoiled brat that he was, I had no other option than to placate him until I could get rid of him for good.

Close to hyperventilating, I breathed in through my nose and out through my mouth, reminding myself to stay calm. I couldn't let this child with scissors, this psychopath with no foresight, make me lose my cool.

"Listen, I understand. You want to see Winter Black off-balance. You want to see her afraid."

"I need her to squirm. I need her to know everything's about to fall apart. All the pieces are in place, and the game is set. And I need it to happen tonight!"

With one last wistful look, I set down my slice of bubbly cheese pizza.

I wanted to hypnotize that dimwit into jumping off a bridge. He'd set me up beautifully to enact the revenge I'd been planning for over a decade, but I didn't need him anymore. I didn't need the stress, and I sure didn't need him pushing me around when I didn't even understand why I was ensnaring the detective. Erik knew all my secrets but never divulged his. I wanted to scream and put my first through the wall. But I had to keep it together.

Erik knew all my secrets.

He knew I'd killed two people already. I was sure he had evidence of it too.

He could end me before my revenge was exacted on the only person who mattered.

"Listen up. No more cross contamination with our vendettas. I'm the Listener, me and only me. And we can find you a code name that's more suiting…um, the Watcher. How does that sound?" Damn, I was good.

"Fine!" he spat into the phone.

That was one small problem solved.

After that, he calmed down and told me where to meet him, promising this next piece of the puzzle would help us both. Which was good or at least necessary. My plan needed to be in the spotlight again, not his stupid threats with the cutout collage. So cliché.

I hung up.

The night wasn't over yet. I was going out. I had more breadcrumbs to drop. Apparently, it wasn't all that hard to get away with murder. You could launch a body off a balcony like you were Tom Brady himself, and the cops wouldn't check the trajectory of the fall. If this next move didn't work, I'd have to take out a billboard with a neon sign, directing the cops to their "killer."

I was not happy.

But once this was over, we'd both be one step closer to our revenge.

29

Perry Bick woke with a start. His heart hammered in his chest, and his forehead was covered in cold sweat.

He'd had night terrors for years, ever since he was a little kid. It wasn't the sort of thing a person got used to. Every new shockwave that came at him in the night was just as powerful as all the others. Often, he couldn't remember why he was so afraid. Dr. Poole told him the terror was a manifestation of his PTSD—repressed memories from his childhood. Nights when he'd wake up cold in his childhood home, his stepfather standing in the doorway and staring.

Perry clenched his eyes shut. He didn't want to remember. Dr. Poole said the brain repressed traumatic memories as a kind of self-defense mechanism, but that it was imperfect. There was no suppressing the subconscious. And pretending the horror had never happened did nothing to heal the pain and panic he carried with him in his body at all times.

Thanks to Dr. Poole, he understood why he was always so afraid to be alone in his bed at night. He'd forgotten more hell in childhood than most people ever encountered their whole lives.

Being in the hospital had been comforting in that sense. He might've been alone in the room, but he could hear the murmur of voices in the hall. Nurses' voices. People who wouldn't hurt him. But his insurance only covered one night before he'd had to go back to the lonely hell of his own bed.

He couldn't remember slitting his wrists…but he could remember why he did it. The man whose name he couldn't remember. The man who would never leave *his* hospital bed. Thoughts of that man overshadowed all other thoughts.

But Winter Black said that memory wasn't real.

Perry's hand was shaking as he reached for the water glass next to the bed, and he took a tremulous sip. How could he go on living in a mind that forgot truths and remembered lies?

Dr. Poole had given him hope that, if he could remember and process the trauma he'd endured, he could live a normal life. Maybe he could finally have a girlfriend—be touched by another person without feeling like his skin was rotting. Maybe he would finally be able to sleep through the night.

But that hope—like every other glimmer he'd ever had—was nothing but a short-lived lie. He was too broken to be normal.

Perry pressed his face into his hands, the bandages on his forearms and wrists scratching against his chin. He wished no one had found him. He wished he'd bled out. Part of him wanted to rip the bandages off and finish the job.

"You were innocent, Perry." Dr. Poole's soothing voice echoed in his head. *"You didn't cause any of what happened to you. You didn't cause it. You were just a child. You are not bad, and you deserve to be happy."*

He wiped the tears from his eyes and found the strength to take another sip of water. All he really wanted was the chance to live and be free of the pain and the panic attacks and the constant triggers that made it so hard to be around other people. He was doing the hard work, after all these years. Finally, he'd found a therapist he could really trust.

But she didn't know about the man he'd nearly killed. Or did she? Had he told her? Did it even happen?

Two days ago, he was absolutely certain it had, but now the story made no sense at all. Perry was too scared to change his clothes in a men's locker room. Whenever he went to the pool to swim laps, he wore his trunks under his pants. He never could've stripped in front of people for money. It was completely absurd.

So why had he accepted it so readily? He didn't know what to believe.

A creak in the hall startled him. Perry's head snapped toward the door, and he froze. A slant of light came in through a crack in the blinds from a streetlamp on the corner. Everything else was pitch dark. He preferred to sleep in the dark. Shadows made faces at him.

Perry reached for the baseball bat he kept next to the bed and swung his legs over the side. He waited in that position for a long time, every muscle tense and ready. He listened to the total emptiness that encapsulated his place. The vague buzz of his refrigerator on the other side of his apartment. And nothing.

With a steadying gulp, Perry rose to his feet. It was nothing, he told himself. But he also knew he wouldn't be able to sleep until he saw the nothing with his own eyes.

With the bat held at the ready, he tiptoed to the edge of his room and drew open the curtain, bathing the bed and edge of the hall in tawny light. Old carpet tickled his bare feet as he stepped into the short hall. From there, he could see straight through to his living room and, beyond that, the kitchen. Two more steps, and he got a look at his front door. Closed.

Perry lowered the bat, letting it hang in his limp hand. He didn't know how much longer he could survive with a brain like his. "Paranoid" was an understatement. He forgot things, made things up, heard noises that weren't there. It was only a matter of time before he started hearing voices. Was he destined to finish out his life talking to himself in a straitjacket?

If straitjackets were even a thing anymore.

Dr. Poole had screened him for schizophrenia and said the tests were negative. Still, maybe they needed to revisit the conversation. He was ready to take any drugs anybody was willing to give him if it meant getting rid of the monsters in his brain.

He went into the bathroom, leaned the bat against the wall, and peed. He didn't want to turn any lights on, knowing that if he did, getting back to sleep would be almost impossible. He'd had insomnia for as long as he could remember. And he was still weak from what he'd done to his wrists the other night. He needed sleep. He needed food. He needed distance from what had happened.

When he was done, he flushed and washed his hands, then went into his room to fetch his water glass for a refill. He reached for it and—

The floor creaked behind him.

Perry whipped around and collided with a hooded figure, sending them stumbling backward. In an instant, they lunged, and Perry drove his elbow into their ribs, more on accident than intent.

A grunt of pain escaped his assailant as they staggered back. A split second later, they were back, fierce and determined. A hot, searing pain seared across Perry's neck.

He flailed wildly, connecting with the figure again, sending them onto his bed.

Clutching his throat, Perry was horrified by the amount of blood gushing from the gash. His attempt to scream was choked off, emerging only as a harsh, wet gurgle.

The attacker quickly regained their footing and lunged again, this time wrapping around him like a koala on a tree. Perry staggered under the unexpected weight, his legs buckling until he collapsed backward onto the bed.

He tried to lift his arm, to shove them off, but his limbs were impossibly heavy, as though they were filling with cement. Powerless, he felt the blade bite into him again. And again. And again.

Why was this happening? What had he ever done to this person?

Blood dripped into his face and eyes, but he didn't even have the energy to blink it away.

The blade entered his throat another time, the fist holding it pounding into his skin. The pressure was there, but the pain was mercifully fading.

I'm dying.

He'd thought about death many times in his life, and especially over the past days and hours. All that time, it'd seemed like a magical escape from the horror and strain of life. Why had he let himself be seduced by that longing, blinded to any joy he might have found?

As the blade entered his skin yet again, an old eighties tune murmured through his mind. "Don't Know What You Got (Till It's Gone)." It was true.

In life, he'd longed for death.

And now, in death, he'd give anything for one more day. One hour. One minute.

One breath.

30

The next morning, as Winter headed out the door to interview Leigh Folke for a second time, she got an unexpected call from Detective Lessner. Her brain swirled with all the reasons he might be calling so early.

Maybe they'd matched the missing letters in the newspaper she found in Dr. Poole's office to the ones in the note she'd received. Maybe they'd found fingerprints. Maybe they'd identified the Caucasian female who had been at the scene when Robin Sheen died.

"Hello?"

"I wanted to give you a courtesy call before you hear about this on the news."

That was not at all what she was expecting or hoping to hear. "What's happened?"

"Your client, Perry Bick, was murdered in his apartment last night."

Murdered? Not suicide?

Winter was standing at her front door, her car keys in hand. She closed it, took a step back, and sank down onto the bench on the porch. "How?"

"Either Perry let the killer into his apartment, or they had a key, because there was no forced entry. They attacked Bick in his bedroom. He was stabbed about a dozen times in the face and neck with a small, sharp object."

"Oh, god…"

"I don't know if you're aware of this, but since you had me tracking the case in Philadelphia, I need to tell you that the M.O. is very similar to that used by the killer in Opal Drewitt's homicide."

His tone made her jaw quiver. She clenched it hard. "What are you saying?"

"Your aunt was stabbed repeatedly in the face and neck. I cannot confirm that the same or similar weapon was used, but it can't be ruled out. Both were small, like a penknife or a scalpel."

Winter's keys fell from her free hand to the ground with a hard smack.

"Since the weapon was small, the killer had to get up close and personal. The number of injuries tells me we're dealing with some kind of serious rage. We aren't officially saying anything's connected, but I'm keeping an open mind. If that turns out to be the case, you need to be careful."

She nodded numbly. Her lips felt swollen. It was hard to speak. "I know."

"For right now, I need you to back off from the blackmail cases. I'm giving all of them higher priority now. My team is on it. Until we can say for certain Perry Bick's homicide isn't connected to Clarissa Toler's or Robin Sheen's suicides—"

"It's all connected."

"—or to Opal Drewitt's homicide, I need you to back off."

"You expect me to…" Arguing would do no good. Maybe with Davenport, but not with Lessner. Even if he was more concerned she'd screw things up by inserting herself into the investigation, he was also worried about her safety now, and rightly so. She had no choice but to capitulate.

"Fine. I'll step back."

That was what she said, but her brain was already churning with what to do next.

31

Noah's running shoes pounded the pavement in rhythm with his racing heart as he headed toward home. Sweat leaked down from his brow to sting his eyes. The buds in his ears played an audiobook read by a British woman that Noah had downloaded only that morning and now was more than halfway through.

"The choice to have a child is not actually a single choice, but hundreds of choices rolled up in one. Would you rather put the kids to bed or go to a party? Go to a restaurant or have friends round? Go on a romantic vacation to Paris or spend the weekend camping in the woods?"

"The comedian Richard Jeni said, 'Choosing to have a child you can't take care of is like farting in an elevator. Sure, you got it out, but now it's everyone else's problem.' Crass as this might sound, the fact of the matter is that it is better to want a child and not have one than to have a child and not want them."

He turned a corner, and his house came into view. His wife was on the porch, her black hair shining vaguely blue in the morning sunlight. At first, he smiled as fantasies filled up his senses. Winter bouncing a baby on her hip as she paced and whispered lullabies. Him taking the child into his arms and telling her to take a nap. Telling her she'd done enough, and he would take it all from here.

Only Winter really was pacing. And instead of a baby in her hands, there was a cell phone, which she kept frantically tapping against her hip bone as she raked the fingers of her other hand through her hair.

Noah paused the book with a click of the button in his ear and padded up onto the porch. "Hey darlin'." He smiled, but she did not return the expression. In fact, now that he was close to her, he could tell she was very upset. "What's the matter?"

"Perry's dead. He was murdered last night in his home. Stabbed in the face and neck with a short knife."

"Shit." Noah lifted the bottom of his shirt and wiped the sweat off his face. He picked up the water bottle he'd left sitting on the porch and took a deep drink, steadying his breathing.

"I just talked to Lessner. He told me to back off, of course. Every damn case, the cops tell me to back off."

A sharp pain twisted in Noah's hamstring. He bent down to stretch. "Well, yeah. What would you tell you if you were in their position?"

She glared at him. "What the hell are you talking about?"

She's not mad at you, old boy. Water off a duck's back.

"If your client's dead, you don't really have a pony in the race, do you?"

"I'm the pony!" Winter jabbed a finger at her own chest. "I was always the pony. The Listener sent me a letter, too, remember?"

"I know. But maybe—"

"Opal was stabbed too. With a little knife. It could be the same person. The same son of a bitch who was pulling Carl Gardner's strings. He's watching me. He's watching us. He put all this together with Clarissa and Robin and Perry just to fuck with me."

Noah wanted to argue with her so badly. He wanted to tell her she was being paranoid. That she ought to just drop the case, let the cops handle it, try to relax. That there was no way anybody would go to such lengths—killing three people—just to screw with her head.

He wanted to say that. He wanted that to be true. But it just wasn't. Not since the Wandering Hearts killer came into their lives. Hell, maybe not since Winter had been born. She wasn't paranoid, and she never had been. Ever since she was a child, people had been coming after her.

"If you think the Listener killed Opal, then I believe you. And I'll be damned if we back off this case before the bastard is behind bars."

Winter's eyes glimmered. She grabbed his hand tightly and squeezed.

"But I'll also be damned if you head out to pound the pavement on your own again while I rot in a damn office. I'm sticking to your ass like glue."

Her entire body sagged with what he could only assume was relief. Lifting up on her tiptoes, she pressed her lips to his cheek. "I'd have it no other way."

❄

They arrived at Leigh Folke's house, their feet crunching on the sandstone gravel as they walked to the door.

Noah was immediately impressed by the look of the place—the epitome of Southwestern chic. He liked the turquoise accent gems in the tall birdbath, the sharp spines of yucca, the puffs of Missouri primrose, and the gorgeous red of the Spanish tile roof. Everything was expertly maintained.

Magic and art could pay pretty good, he supposed.

Though he imagined that probably wasn't true for most people. Maybe there was something to that. If Leigh Folke turned out to be the Listener, they might just find out this hadn't been her first rodeo when it came to blackmail. Somebody like her—who had led such an eclectic, bohemian life—probably knew a lot of secrets.

Noah followed along behind Winter, vaguely chastising himself for appreciating the way her ass swayed as she walked. She was possessed of laser-like focus, ignoring everything, including him. She made a beeline for the solid pine door with the little stained-glass window near the top and pounded with her fist.

The sound snapped him into focus like a dog hearing a whistle. Noah set his hand on his hip right near his gun as he sauntered up behind her. His muscles were loose, his heart keeping a steady and quick rhythm. He was ready for anything.

At the sound of shuffling inside, Noah widened his stance. A moment later, a small woman pulled open the door. She was dressed in a long robe, a towel turban on her head. She scanned Winter and frowned, then glanced at Noah and straightened.

"*A macska rúgja meg.*" Noah didn't know a lot of Hungarian, but he'd heard the phrase before. *May the cat kick it* was a very weird way of cursing. "Winter Black. What do you want now?"

Winter jutted her chin in the air. "Leigh Folke. Have you heard?"

"Heard what?"

"Two more of Dr. Poole's patients are dead. Perry Bick and Robin Sheen. Two patients who both received blackmail threats."

Leigh's square shoulders slumped as her body deflated. Noah knew that tell. The woman was hiding something.

"And you seemed to know that Clarissa Toler was being blackmailed as well."

"So?"

"So..." Winter drew out the word, kindling the moment. "The police never released that information. And it's not the kind of thing one talks about in a waiting room."

Leigh's eyes got wide before she lowered her gaze, her posture drooping even more. She might've collapsed into a puddle if her claw-like hand hadn't been clutching the doorjamb.

"Fine." She turned and headed back into her house. "Come inside."

Winter caught Noah's eye, and he nodded. They followed her in as he shut the door behind them.

Leigh's house smelled of patchouli and chai. The old hardwood floor looked freshly polished, the walls draped in art and macramé. A large hutch on the far wall with glass doors was filled with treasures from a well-traveled life. And sitting on a perfectly appointed silk pillow in one corner was a large and extremely fluffy white cat. The creature glared at them in contempt as they moved toward a collection of antique chairs and took a seat where Folke indicated.

"I lied to you yesterday." Leigh perched on the corner of a golden chaise lounge.

Noah watched as Winter's icy blue stare bore into her. "I noticed."

"I did get a letter. A vague, pointless, stupid letter threatening that I would end up like Clarissa if I didn't pay up."

"Where is it, Leigh?" Noah asked.

"Probably in the city dump by now. The second I received it, I ripped it up and threw it away. Who are you?"

"Noah Dalton with Black Investigations. Why didn't you report it?"

Leigh gave him a haughty look. "Because I don't give a damn. What could they dredge up against me that I wouldn't freely admit to? Yes, I've lived a colorful life. And yes, I've done dozens of things that I'm not proud of. But haven't we all? I'm an artist, not a politician. I've had lots of sex. I've done lots of drugs. Who cares?"

Winter looked at Noah, and her eye twitched. "So why lie about it?"

For the first time, Leigh looked a little sheepish. "I found my letter the same night Clarissa died. When it said I'd end up like her, I had no idea what it meant at the time. It was only the next morning that I saw she'd been killed."

"Killed herself, you mean."

Leigh shook her head. "I'll never believe that. Listen, I knew Clarissa, outside of Poole's office. We were friends."

"How did you know her?"

"We met at a children's arts festival a couple years back. We weren't super close, but we ran in a lot of the same circles downtown." Leigh's expression softened. "We both hated small talk with a blinding passion, so whenever we got together, we'd end up just talking about big stuff. And especially when we figured out that we were both going to the same therapist, we'd get together for coffee sometimes and talk about our traumas, our mental disorders. Hypnotism. All that kind of stuff."

Leigh stood and went to a small table in the corner where she took a tissue from a box and dabbed at her eyes. Noah hadn't been in Austin long, but he knew the artist community was tight-knit, just from going out into the city but also from all his recent research. And he sensed true remorse emanating from the woman before them.

"She was such a sweet person. And I knew she wouldn't have killed herself, not like that. And not without leaving a note. The woman was a writer, for crying out loud."

Winter's body ease a bit, and Noah knew something in Leigh's story had slipped through her thick outer walls and into her soft marshmallow of a heart. "If she was your friend and you suspected somebody might have murdered her, why keep it all to yourself? Why not call the police and tell them what you think? Don't you want her killer brought to justice?"

"How dare you judge me?" Leigh clenched a fist around the tissue. "You don't know what I've been through. You don't know anything about me. And you sure as hell don't know what it's like to realize some psycho who just killed your friend is threatening to do the same to you."

Noah watched Winter, wondering how she might respond to that erroneous accusation. Unfortunately, his wife knew better than anyone what it was like to live with constant threats from the shadows. Hell, she was dealing with the same fears Leigh was currently.

She was chewing on the inside of her lip. "I take it you didn't bother to google me after our last visit?"

Leigh's eyes widened, as if she'd been caught stealing from a cookie jar. Then she waved a dismissive hand. "You win. I guess we're all pretty fucked up, huh?"

"I wanted to ask you about the time you spent working in Vegas." Noah scanned the room, looking for any clues, but there were too many tchotchkes, so much art. The house was like a crowded museum. It would take days to understand just what he was looking at.

Leigh sighed with exhaustion. "What about it?"

"Were you a part of a magic show?"

She shook her head and flicked her gaze toward two oversize feather fans hanging on one wall. "Cabaret and burlesque. The choreographer by that point. I'm a woman of many talents."

He didn't doubt that. "This is a very nice house you have here. There must be a lot of money in burlesque."

Leigh snorted. "There's a lot of money in ex-husbands. Trust me, I have three. I couldn't possibly recommend it more."

Noah eyed Winter and gave her a small nod, indicating he was ready to go if she was.

She hopped up from her seat, took a card from her pocket, and held it out to Leigh. "If you hear from the Listener again, you need to contact us immediately."

"I suppose you're going to tell the police about the letter I received." Leigh took the card.

"Don't be surprised if the police show up here later today to ask you some questions about it. I highly recommend not leaving town."

With that, Noah thanked Leigh for her help, and they left. Neither one of them said a word to the other until they were off Leigh Folke's property and sequestered inside Beaulah, Noah's giant truck.

"Do you think she's lying?"

"No." Winter shook her head. "Now, do I think she's telling the whole truth? No." She sighed and folded over her own lap. "But I don't think she's the Listener."

"Me neither." He fired up the engine and put her into gear. "That doesn't leave a lot of options."

"Dr. Poole's?"

"Shall we head over to her office and see what the old gal has to say for herself?"

"I'm not sure I see the point. She's usually about as helpful as a cactus shoved down your pajamas."

"Maybe I can get her to talk." Noah popped on his sunglasses and eased the truck out onto the street. "I've got a way with women, you know."

32

When they pulled up to Dr. Poole's office, Winter was surprised to see three police cruisers parked in the lot with blue-and-red lights whirling and several uniforms milling about the grounds. Cybil was standing off to one side with two cops, her arms folded across her chest and her eyes downcast as she spoke with them.

Noah parked on the street, but Winter hopped out of the truck before he even set the parking brake. As she jogged toward the scene, Lessner emerged from the office. Behind him, two uniformed officers were leading Dr. Poole out, her hands cuffed behind her back.

Winter's lips parted. For a while, she watched in silence, her mind strangely blank, as they placed a frightened-looking Dr. Poole into the back of a cruiser. Lessner stood beside the SUV, scribbling on a clipboard before handing it off to someone else.

When he lifted his gaze, he saw Winter. His bulldog face didn't change. He always looked a bit angry and disappointed, but he sighed and shook his head slightly before he began to approach her.

Winter hurried forward to meet him. "What happened? You got something on her?"

"Computer forensics finally tracked down whose email address was associated with the Paymo account listed in the blackmail demands…" He glanced around and lowered his voice. "The judge signed the warrant half an hour ago. So once we compare her DNA to the hair found on Robin Sheen…"

"So it was Poole…" Winter's gaze was locked on the cruiser she knew contained the doctor, even if the tinted windows prevented her from seeing inside.

"Who else could it have been? And there's likely DNA at Bick's. *The Listener Was Here* was scrawled across the bathroom mirror in what looks to be red lipstick. It seems you were on to something with the whole hypnosis angle." He sniffed deeply and set his hands on his hips. "Look, I ain't got time for chitchat. And you're not supposed to be here anyway. I told you to back off."

Winter chose not to acknowledge that. "Did she say anything when you came for her?"

"You mean, did she confess?" Lessner shook his head. "She tried to show us a letter she supposedly received, but of course she'd say that. Forensics won't lie."

Winter didn't argue, and a moment later, Lessner walked away from her and back into his official investigation.

So she was right. Dr. Poole was the killer—the talented hypnotist so adept at mind control, she could literally talk someone into taking their own life. And now she'd be behind bars, likely to never reemerge into society.

The danger was over, and the monster was gone. So why did Winter still feel like someone was watching her?

33

I didn't believe in the death penalty. Not because I was worried about hurting innocent people or thought it was barbaric or bought into the naive fiction that we lived in a just society. I did not. Death came to everyone and could even be sweet and welcoming for some. And that was why I didn't believe in death as a punishment.

Some people deserved worse.

They deserved to watch everything they've ever worked for crumble all around them. They deserved to be publicly maligned and ostracized and despised. They deserved to be locked up like animals, fed disgusting food, tortured by sadists. They deserved to have their faces smeared all over the internet so everybody who'd ever respected them came to despise them. They deserved to spend their entire lives in an American prison—a fate worse than death.

Let them live.

Let them suffer.

Simply killing the monster who ruined my life would have been pathetically insufficient. Death was too good for someone like that. I had to completely destroy her—frighten her, publicly humiliate her, watch her beg for mercy.

Dr. Poole was finally going to receive her deserved punishment, the punishment I'd spent my whole adult life planning. I'd carefully woven together every thread of her demise, framing her for murders committed in such a way that any reasonable person would suspect a mental health expert of committing the crimes.

Nobody would ever take a second glance at little old me. What could I possibly know about the mind? I didn't have degrees on top of degrees gracing any of my walls.

No, she was the pro.

I'd often wondered if Dr. Poole had compelled my father to have an affair with her. If she'd dug her hypnotic claws into his mind to transform him from a good man into a lying, cheating monster. That single question pushed me to learn everything there was to know about her field of study —hypnotism and the subconscious.

Somewhere along the way, I realized that if I were ever going to get revenge on Dr. Poole, I'd have to beat her at her own game. I had to become the best there was at hypnotism because, one day, I'd use it to destroy her.

It took the cops longer than I'd anticipated to track her down. I thought the Paymo account that Erik registered to one of Poole's rarely used personal email addresses would be enough.

Instead, I had to lead the pigs by the nose to the scene of a crime by leaving some of Dr. Poole's hair—stolen from the brush she kept in her desk—in Robin's car. And then a damn note at Perry's! I had Poole's cherry-red lipstick on hand just in case. More DNA. More proof. It was Erik's idea, of course, but I put my own spin on the message. Erik was not going to be happy.

Like I cared.

The cops let me leave the scene just after Poole was arrested. They tried to interview me, but I was too upset. Crying, shaking. Poor me, I didn't know anything. I'd only started to work there three months ago. What did I know about the secret life of Ava Poole? Nothing.

They asked me about the burglary, and I told them what I knew. That Dr. Poole told me it had happened after she'd worked late and left the door unlocked. How she begged me not to report it because she could get in big trouble.

I was so scared I'd lose my job. And I was all alone in this city, my only family, an aunt, still out in California. Pitiful, sad girl. I was so sorry. I should've known better. It was my fault Perry Bick and Clarissa Toler and Robin Sheen were dead. How could I be so stupid? Sob, sob, sob. Poor me.

The cop bought my little skit hook, line, and sinker. He gave me a tissue and a bottle of water, all the while looking down my blouse. Just like a man. The only thing worse than disgusting men were the women who let them get away with it. Women who encouraged them and didn't care who they hurt along the way.

Women like Dr. Ava Poole.

I drove straight home after the cops let me leave. My heart was like a kick drum in my chest, my skin tight and tingly. I couldn't tell if I was anxious or excited. Ecstatic, I supposed. The kind of happiness so intense, it was scary, even painful. I'd never experienced anything like it. But for how long I'd worked and how much I'd sacrificed, I deserved every delicious drop of this feeling.

I went inside and flung myself on the sofa. The minute I was alone, hysterical laughter broke from my chest. At last. It was done. I was free.

My phone started ringing, "Shut Up and Let Me Go"

cutting into my reverie like a needle plunged into my eye. I snatched it up and glared at Erik's name.

But even that made me smile. I was done with him too. He'd helped me in the beginning. I didn't know how he did it exactly, but he got rid of Dr. Poole's old receptionist so I could take her place. I had a horrible feeling the woman was dead. But I slid into Dr. Poole's life the week that assistant went away. I ran right into her at her favorite deli…

"Dr. Poole, is that you? It's me, Cybil. Dennis Johnston's daughter."

You should've seen the look on her face. She'd been terrified. I'd watched guilt rush up her neck and redden her entire face.

Yes, Dr. Poole. I'm your worst nightmare all grown up. A reminder of what a loathsome excuse for a human you are.

And then I'd hugged her. It was a reunion, over ten years in the making. And I held on tight until that skin-and-bones bitch hugged me back.

We got to talking after that, as "old friends" did. And I casually mentioned my degree in psychology, my interest in neuroscience. How she'd inspired it all.

"What's that, you say, Dr. Poole? There's an opening in your office for a receptionist?"

How she'd jumped at the chance to hire me when I told her I was between jobs and that the timing was serendipitous. It was as if I were the Pope himself, washing away all her sins. She thought hiring me would absolve her, erase what she'd done to my family, to my mother.

"How is your father, by the way?" She'd slipped her question in at the end of the conversation, as if she hadn't been working up the courage the whole time we'd been talking.

"He's great. I'll tell him you said hi." I'd smiled wide as the lie slipped between my teeth.

People were so fucking easy to fool. Her life just went on after she destroyed ours. She didn't even look back to see what she'd done. The lives she'd taken. The childhood she'd destroyed. She was no better than a weasely, selfish, hit-and-run driver.

The very next day, I'd started working in her office.

I watched as Erik's call finally went to voicemail before tossing my phone aside. I was tired of Erik and his cryptic nonsense. His weird obsessions. His stupid voice. When I'd agreed to work with him, I had no idea just how needy he was going to be. Calling and texting and emailing all the time, even showing up at my house.

I asked him once why he was so pathetically codependent and offered him a book full of strategies on how to get over it. That made him very, very mad, which was sort of the point. Still, he should've read it. It would have done him good.

Dr. Ava Poole was about to get her just deserts, but Erik wasn't going to let himself be ignored. If he showed up here —when he showed up here—I would have to deal with him.

Maybe I'd pull that same knife he'd given me to use on Perry, provided I could get the jump on him. He'd been very particular that I use that knife for a death by stabbing. Something to drive Winter crazy, I supposed. I didn't understand, and I didn't want to.

"Stab him! Stab him twelve times. In the neck!" Of course, with his damn angry repetitive stutter, it came out, *"Stab him! Stab stab stab him twelve times in the neck!"*

Yeah, yeah, I heard ya the first time.

"Then add a note to the mirror that the Watcher was here."

I'd done as I was told, mostly. But he wasn't getting credit for all that work. Besides, I had to ensure Dr. Poole would go down.

It was the Listener who was there, nut bag, not the Watcher. You want credit, you wield the knife.

I'd held up my half of the bargain. Now it was time for Erik and me to part ways. I had my whole life ahead. And at long last, I was finally ready to live it.

34

Back at the office, Winter sat down at the table in the break room and warmed her clammy hands on a fresh cup of coffee. She kept waiting for a wave of relief to wash over her. The Listener was in custody. The monster who killed her own patients—Clarissa Toler, Robin Sheen, Perry Bick. Maybe even Opal. Her spree was finally at an end, and the nightmare was over.

But Winter didn't feel any better. If anything, watching the psychologist led away in handcuffs had made her feel worse. The pit in her stomach was growing, the knots in her back only getting tighter.

Dr. Poole was the obvious suspect. Material evidence was found at two of the murder scenes, connecting her to the crimes. Her email address was associated with the online account referenced in all the blackmail demands. And the way Clarissa Toler and Robin Sheen had been killed— hypnotized into taking their own lives—was a giant flashing arrow pointing right at the doctor.

And, of course, the cut-up newspaper used to create the threatening letter Winter received had been left in her office.

Dr. Ava Poole was a lot of things—secretive, unpleasant, self-absorbed. And maybe she was even a murderer.

But she wasn't stupid.

"It's like she was trying to get caught." Winter drummed her fingers on the warm ceramic mug.

Noah returned from his trip to the bathroom and bypassed Winter, going straight for the fridge. He rooted around for a few minutes, groaning quietly at the mostly empty shelves.

"If Dr. Poole wanted money, why would she have pushed her targets to kill themselves? Why would she have violently attacked Perry?"

Noah stood up and rested against the countertop. He plucked a lonely orange from the fruit bowl and poked at the peel with a stubby fingernail. "She realized none of them were going to pay up?"

"Blackmailers usually just go ahead and air their victims' dirty laundry in that case."

"Right, except she didn't actually have anything on any of them," Noah countered, effortlessly settling into his role as devil's advocate. "She was blackmailing them over the false memories she'd implanted."

"Another giant glowing arrow pointing right at her head." Finishing the last of her coffee, Winter slammed down the mug, rose to her feet, and started to pace. "Dr. Poole must have tons of patients. If she needed money, couldn't she have just picked some that she had real, actual dirt on and blackmailed them? Why bother implanting memories?"

Noah rolled the unpeeled orange between his palms. "Maybe these victims were easier to influence than the others. Maybe it's a power thing. She wanted to see if she really could hypnotize someone into taking their own lives."

Winter cringed at the hideousness of that theory, though she had to admit it was plausible. "Why not do that quietly, then? Why bother with this trail of blackmail leading right back to herself?"

"Okay." Noah pinched at the skin of the orange, trying to pop it open. "So she implants the false memory and sends the blackmail letter because she wants to test just how deeply she can penetrate the person's brain. Do they believe in the lie deeply enough to actually kill themselves over it?"

Winter snatched the orange, dug her sharp fingernail under the skin to get it started, and handed it back to him. "Okay, so Dr. Poole's on a power trip. She's experimenting with her patients. Changing their memories, talking them into things, controlling them with her mind tricks."

"She has a god complex." Noah shoved a section of orange into his cheek and talked through it. "And like so many people who think they're smarter than everybody else, she started making careless mistakes. The Paymo account, the newspaper…"

"What about the robbery? Why go to the trouble of stealing your own patients' files to take the heat off yourself but then not report it?" Winter shook her head, still pacing in a small circle around the break room. "That makes no sense. That's not a careless mistake. It's just pointlessly stupid."

"And we've established that Dr. Poole is not stupid."

"If Dr. Ava Poole wanted to play god with her patients, she could've easily gotten away with it." The words came out of her mouth before Winter fully understood their implications.

"Maybe she's been doing it for years, darlin'."

She shivered at the thought, especially knowing Dr. Poole specialized in working with PTSD—traumatized individuals who already had so much difficulty trusting anybody or anything.

"Maybe," Noah went on, "if we spoke to her other patients and investigated their pasts, we'd find hundreds of false memories. For all we know, she's been running an unethical case study for the last decade. If her passion for hypnotherapy is stronger than her oath to do no harm, they're truly just test subjects to her."

"Maybe..." Winter slumped back into her chair. The energy that had animated her a moment ago felt like it had all drained away, like someone had pulled a plug in her soul. She had PTSD, both from her own traumatic childhood and from events she'd experienced as an adult. Noah did too.

Winter had resisted working with a therapist. Well, other than her best friend, Autumn Trent. But that didn't really count.

The idea of opening up her old wounds and poking around inside was about as appealing as jumping into a barrel of ice water. She imagined it was a feeling shared by many individuals with her condition.

It took a lot of courage for someone with trauma to face the facts and ask for help. The idea of a professional abusing that trust and treating her patients like a bunch of lab rats made her nauseous.

"I looked into Dr. Poole's past." Noah's deep, soothing voice pulled Winter back from her rumination. "It's very possible I missed something, but I didn't find any complaints from other patients." He tossed the orange peels in the garbage. "And I couldn't find any connection between you and her." He popped another orange slice into his mouth. "What I don't understand is the fake flyers alongside every blackmail demand. Why? Plus, she didn't even try to make them seem real."

Winter chewed on her bottom lip. "She didn't want me implicated. She just wanted me interested."

"Exactly. Why? Why would anybody trying to conceal a crime go out of their way to make sure Winter Black became aware of it? Why would anyone threatening to blackmail and kill their own patients direct those same patients to you?"

"It's a game. Like the letter said. I'm the player, and this is a labyrinth that's been set up for me to walk through." She slid back into a chair at the table.

"That's a lot of effort for minimal reward. Now that she's in custody, she can't exactly keep the game going. Maybe she's just another pawn in somebody else's game."

"You think she's been framed?" Winter had been wondering the same thing.

Noah sat across from her. "Let's pretend that she is. That Dr. Poole had nothing to do with any of this and, instead, has been set up to take the fall. How does that change things?"

"It changes everything." Winter's foot twitched, electricity building in her blood once again. "If Dr. Poole's innocent, that means somebody else had access to all her patients."

"Cybil Kerie."

"Or Leigh Folke. We can't rule her out just yet."

"Okay. But why would either one of them want to hurt Dr. Poole?"

"Folke can't seem to stand the woman." Winter dragged her fingers through her hair. "And Cybil doesn't like her either."

"And both women could be theoretically capable of hypnotizing a person, if you think about it. But committing murder and framing Dr. Poole? That's a big leap."

Winter jerked up so hard and fast, she hit her knees on the table. "Dr. Poole denied having any knowledge that her files had been burglarized. I thought she was lying, but maybe she was telling the truth."

"Okay, let's say she was telling the truth. What does that mean?"

"Cybil was lying."

He cocked an eyebrow. "Why would she do that?"

"To put more suspicion on Dr. Poole." Something was circling in Winter's brain, just out of reach. "Cybil clearly has an axe to grind with Dr. Poole. She doesn't like her at all. She even went so far as to say her therapy methods were sketchy. And Cybil had access to all Dr. Poole's files, all her patients."

"So if Cybil framed Dr. Poole for murder, the question remains…why?"

Winter's eye twitched, snippets of her interactions with Cybil springing up and splashing all through her brain. She squeezed both her eyes shut tight, and the missing piece fell into place.

Her eyes flew open. She hadn't seen it earlier when the two of them had commiserated over the sad stories of their lives, but now it was clear.

"I know why."

35

I took one last look around my apartment. Though I'd only lived in it for three months, there was something special about this place. I'd moved closer to Blue Tree Wellness when I got hired so I didn't need to waste time with a commute. This was the place where I finally came into myself. Where I stopped being a victim. Where I found justice after all these years.

I was going to miss this place. But I was also relieved it was all finally over. The best way to tie up my loose ends was simply to sever them. After all, with Dr. Poole in jail, I didn't have a job anymore. I didn't even need to stay in Austin. I could move anywhere. Be anything.

Giggles bubbled up my throat. I'd laughed more today than I had in ten years. It felt so good, so freeing.

Yes. It was time to leave Texas forever.

I'd called my aunt in California earlier, and she'd agreed to let me stay in her mother-in-law apartment while I looked for a new job. I'd hoped to weasel some money out of this deal with Erik, but that hadn't ended up happening. And I'd promised myself I wouldn't get hung up on the blackmail aspect of my suicide scheme.

Still, it was a little disappointing. One or two counts of murder would've been plenty to lock Dr. Poole up for life. And fifteen grand—the fifty-fifty split Erik and I agreed to, should one of them pay up—would've been really nice, but it wasn't my fault the pigs were like Dumb and Dumber when it came to solving crimes.

Oh, well. You can't have it all.

I had enough money to travel to my aunt's, and it'd be good for me to settle into a regular job again right away. I'd figure it out. I always did.

"A normal life." That sounded strange to my ears but really comforting. Now that Dr. Ava Poole had finally gotten the punishment she so desperately deserved, I could finally have one of those. I couldn't wait.

I gripped the handle of my roller bag. I had no plans of waiting until morning. I didn't have a job to go to, anyway, and I was done dealing with Erik. It was time to go.

My phone started to play that damn song again. Erik, of course. He'd been calling me every ten minutes, ever since Dr. Poole got arrested. A part of me still wondered if I ought to just finish him off. I'd actually tried to hypnotize Erik, but it turned out he was in the majority of the population and not at all susceptible to it.

Denied the opportunity to mesmerize his mind, I was afraid to go after him. I was a tiny woman, after all. And while Erik might not have been big like Robin or in shape like Perry, he was exceptionally violent and thoroughly crazy.

The stories he told me sent shivers down my spine. The way he spoke of his intentions for Winter Black. All his plans for "leveling himself up" before the "final boss battle" and the traps he intended to lay.

His game brain was toast, severed from reality. And, I swore, if I had to see him in that stupid t-shirt one more time —with the six video game controllers that said *Check Out My Six-Pack*—I was going to tear it off his body and set it on fire.

I glared at the phone as it went to voicemail, but it almost immediately started playing The Ting Tings again.

"Just shut up!" I yelled before answering the phone. "What do you want?"

"Where do you think you're going?"

Just by the sound of his voice, I could tell he was already all geared up.

"It's over, Erik. I'm going back to California."

"Like hell! We're not done yet."

I paced over to the window. "You're not done. I'm done."

"That is not how this works. My target is still active. We had a deal."

"I did everything you asked me to. All you did was get some bitch fired so I could take her job. I killed a man with a damn pen knife!"

"I didn't get anyone fired."

Shit. I knew it. I stumbled over that, my focus darting around my apartment as all my nostalgia for the place vanished. Suddenly, the walls looked eerie, like they were closing in. "Convinced her to quit, whatever."

"She's dead, Cybil."

Shit, shit, shit. And she meant nothing to him. What did that mean for me?

I pulled my voice down a notch. "Look, I appreciate whatever you did for me. But I've done a lot for you in return. It's over now."

"It's not over! I know about the lipstick. I know what you wrote. And I told you to leave that note for Winter Black. For Winter! From me! From the Watcher!"

"So first you want me to take all the blame, and you sign

my code name without my permission to Winter's dumb cutout note, and now you're eight ways to angry because I took credit for the crime I actually committed?" I stomped my foot, even though he couldn't see or hear it. "That doesn't even make sense!"

"The note was my idea. The murder was my idea. Now Winter doesn't know I was there. You made me look like a fucking noob!"

"You weren't there!" I was so over his gamer talk. "This needed to be clear to take Dr. Poole down. It needed to be the Listener!"

"Oh, I was there, Cybil. In spirit! You'll see."

"Well, listen up, Mr. Watcher, the Listener's gotta get the hell out of Dodge before anybody catches on."

"That's not how this works!" he shrieked, and I had to yank the phone away from my ear. "We had a deal!"

"Fuck your deal! And fuck you, too, Erik!" I ended the call. My shoulders rose and fell with every frantic breath. Then, suddenly, every hair on my body stood on end.

How the hell did he know I was leaving? I hadn't said a word.

My phone dinged with a text. Erik. Clenching my teeth, I swiped it open and watched in horror as a short video played back.

Me standing in my apartment next to my suitcase, screaming at my phone. I was in live time for Erik's viewing pleasure.

The Watcher. I should've known. I'd named the nut bag, after all.

His video was angled at about hip height from across my apartment. He'd installed a camera somewhere in my living room. Maybe in the entertainment center. How long had it been there? How many of them were there? It felt like ants were biting me everywhere. That psycho. He'd gone too far.

How much of my life had he been filming? Did he record me printing out the fake flyers for Winter Black's offices? Typing up the blackmail letters? Did he have footage of me coming home after killing Perry and cleaning off the bloody knife?

Just as I was scanning for tiny cameras, a knock interrupted my focus, and I nearly jumped out of my skin. I ran to the kitchen and snatched up a French butcher knife, brandishing it like a sword. If Erik wanted a fight, then I was going to give him one.

In 4D, you little punk. See how you like that!

I wasn't very strong, but I was fast. If he attacked me, I wouldn't hesitate to go for the throat. Hell, I was all practiced up.

"Cybil?" a woman's voice called from the other side of the door. It was Winter Black.

What the hell did she want?

"I know you're in there, Cybil. I can see your shadow moving."

I glared at the frosted glass window in the door. I knew I should've blacked that out.

Cursing under my breath, I glanced around. I was up on the fourth floor, so there was no way out. If I tried to go out a window, I'd end up like Clarissa.

"I know what you did, Cybil. I know you set up Dr. Poole." Her fist pounded against the door again. "I know why you did it. You told me why you did it. Your father cheated on your mother and left her for another woman. Ruined your family. Dr. Poole was the other woman."

Hearing those words out loud was like somebody driving chopsticks into my ears.

"Your mother killed herself. When you moved in with your father, it was on the heels of Dr. Poole dumping him, and he started drinking all the time. And then he died, too, when he wrapped his truck around a tree."

I clamped my hands over my ears. "Shut up!"

"You lost both your parents. You were left all alone and had to fend for yourself. And you blamed Dr. Poole for that."

This wasn't happening. This couldn't be happening. I was seconds away from getting out of this godforsaken place.

"Ava Poole got exactly what she deserved!" The words were like razors to my throat.

"And what about Clarissa? And Robin? And Perry? Did they get what they deserved?"

That was Erik's fault. He forced me to get Winter involved in all this.

"There's no way out, Cybil." Winter knocked again, more gently this time. "Open the door, please."

No way out. That was the story of my life. But I looked at the knife in my hand, and I knew she was wrong. There was always a way out.

I stepped up to the door and undid the lock.

36

Winter was surprised when the lock turned and the door popped open an inch.

For all her bravado, they had no hard evidence connecting Cybil to the crimes. She knew Cybil's motive, though, because she'd freely admitted it. Well, that, and some corroborating evidence Noah had found of Dr. Poole being brought in on an ethics violation for sleeping with one of her patients.

The man was Dennis Johnston, married to Kerie Johnston. Her father left the family for Dr. Ava Poole, creating a spiral effect that led to Kerie Johnston's death by suicide. But eventually, Dr. Poole had to choose between her lover and her career. She picked her career and broke the man's heart.

By eighteen, with both parents deceased, Cybil changed her last name to her mother's first name, ridding herself of any association with her late father. Or so she thought.

It was clear Cybil blamed Dr. Poole for ripping her family apart—Winter had discerned that the moment she'd heard Cybil's story, even though she hadn't known yet that the other woman had been Dr. Poole. And when Noah had looked into her background, they'd discovered that Cybil had an undergrad in psychology and was halfway to a master's when she'd dropped out.

She'd studied the human mind. She knew how it worked. And she had access to all of Dr. Poole's patient files.

It all made sense. But if they were to convict Cybil Kerie of murdering Clarissa Toler, Robin Sheen, and Perry Bick, they needed more than motive, opportunity, and a half-assed, through-the-door acknowledgment of the crimes. They needed a real confession.

Noah stood at Winter's back, holding his gun low so Cybil wouldn't see it. Winter felt confident with him there, like nothing could touch her. In fact, she hadn't felt this safe in a long time.

Her own gun was tucked in the back of her belt. Just in case.

Winter pushed the door open with the tip of her foot.

Cybil stood before them, somehow looking smaller than ever, her skin pale except right around her eyes, where it was bright red. Her hair hung loose and tangled around her shoulders. Shadows caressed her downcast face. In one hand, she held a kitchen knife with about a ten-inch blade.

"You win." Cybil's words moved through the apartment like a ghost. "I'm the Listener."

Winter took a step inside, Noah close at her back.

Cybil's whole body lifted and fell with each heavy, exhausted breath. "I'm not sorry for what I did, though, Winter. You weren't there. You didn't see what she did to my mother."

"I understand—"

"No, you don't. You can't. I was a kid. First, I watched my daddy leave me. Then I had to watch my mother as she sank deeper and deeper into depression." Her eyes grew rounder and redder as she spoke. "She stopped cleaning, stopped taking me to school. There was no food in the house. I had to look after myself. And I tried to look after her."

Winter didn't want to envision what she was saying, but she couldn't help it. When she and Noah had looked deeper into Cybil's past, they'd learned her parents were divorced by the time Cybil was eleven, and her mother died when she was only thirteen.

"She told me why my father left. That he loved a stranger more than either of us. And then one day, I came home and found my mom laid out on her bed in a puddle of vomit. She wasn't moving. I tried to wake her up, over and over." Her voice choked with a noise like tears, but her hand only tightened on the knife.

"I'm so sorry that happened to you."

"I had to go live with my father. Dr. Poole had just left him. She broke up my family, stole my father, and threw him away like he was nothing." Her teeth clenched in anger. "All he did was drink and drink. I tried to take care of him too. To make him feel better."

"It was never your job to look after him. Or your mom. There was nothing you could've done."

"I think he killed himself too. I think he hit that tree on purpose." Tears slid down her cheeks. "Because of that bitch. Because she seduced him and broke his heart."

"Why go to all this trouble? If your problem was with Dr. Poole, why not just go after her?"

"Because death is too good for her." Cybil's eyes snapped wide open, dark and wild as a gathering thunderstorm. "She deserves to suffer for what she did. Like I've suffered."

"And what about Clarissa? And Robin? And Perry? What did they ever do to you?"

Cybil shook her head but didn't say a word. She looked back down at her toes.

"They had families, too, you know. People who loved them. People whose lives now have big gaping holes in them because they're gone. Did you think about them at all? Or were they just collateral damage?"

"Yes. They were. They don't matter."

Winter felt so sick to her stomach, she had to set a hand on it.

"It's over, Cybil." Noah's voice was deep and certain. "You need to go to the police and tell them the truth. It's your only hope of getting some leniency. If you confess, there's a good chance they'll take the death penalty off the table."

"I'd rather die!" Cybil barked the words at them. She was visibly shaking all over.

"Why did you involve me in all this?" Winter pressed her hands to her sides. "Are you part of Justin's fan club?"

"What?" The confusion on her face seemed genuine.

"Why did you send out those flyers? Why did you send me threatening notes?" Winter swallowed a hard lump in her throat. "Are you the one who's been watching me? Are you the one who killed my aunt?"

Cybil pressed a hand to her temple. "No. It would've been a lot better for me if you were never involved."

"What do you mean, 'no?' You're the Listener, aren't you?" Then Winter played her trump card. "The knife that killed Perry is the same one that killed my aunt."

Cybil stared at Winter, her jaw slack with shock. Seconds passed as the young woman processed the information.

"Oh." Her nostrils flared. "That makes sense."

"What makes sense?" Winter was getting angry now, fire burning in her frontal lobe.

"That wasn't me." Cybil jerked her chin up, her eyes blazing now. "That was all him. The Watcher."

37

"Him?" The word was a stiletto to Winter's gut. She almost physically lurched before she caught herself. "Who?"

Cybil pursed her lips. She searched Winter's face, her gaze red-hot. "You know what, Winter? I kind of like you. And I fucking hate him, so I'm going to tell you the truth."

Noah's shoulder touched the back of hers, a silent bit of support. She glanced back at him to see his eyes were focused, his face furrowed and intense.

"Tell us. Who's Winter's stalker? Who's the Watcher person?"

"His name is Erik Saulson. And he hates you at least as much as I hate Dr. Poole. He never said why, though. And trust me, I've asked."

"Erik," Noah echoed before releasing a string of curses. "The man in the park. My height, beard? Crazy eyes."

Cybil looked past Winter to Noah. "Oh, yeah, that's him. But he's not your height. He must've had those dumb boots on with the heels. Thinks he's so clever. He did say he made a point of running into you. Said he wanted to look into the eyes of the attack dog before he put it down for good." She shrugged. "I first met Erik online in a chat room for haters."

Winter was confused. She waited a moment for the rest of the sentence. "Haters. People who hate what?"

"Everything!" Cybil shouted. Then she laughed. The cold sound bounced off the empty walls of her apartment. "People who've been ruined. People who want revenge. I told him all about Dr. Poole, and we agreed to help each other."

"How?" Winter caught Noah in her periphery again. Her heart was on fire.

"He told me about his special skills. Spying, planning, organization, tech stuff. And I told him about mine."

"And what's that?"

"Hypnosis, of course. I started learning how to do it way back in high school. I experimented on this shy, weak-willed, pathetic girl who thought I was her friend. I hypnotized her and got her to take her clothes off in the lunchroom in front of everybody."

Cybil sounded proud, like she was enumerating her accomplishments for a job interview.

Her mouth curved into a cruel smile at the memory. "And then I got more schooling. And I've been taking advantage of vulnerable idiots ever since. Erik was the definition of preparation meeting opportunity."

They weren't even people to Cybil, Winter realized, the twist in her gut growing steadily worse. It was like she gauged whether a person was worthy of any respect by how easy it was to manipulate them.

"Erik challenged me, asked if I could hypnotize someone into killing themselves. I said of course I could. And he said that was all he needed to know. Then he helped me get a job at Dr. Poole's office. He told me to find a handful of patients I could easily control and prep them for later use. He told me the best way to destroy a person wasn't to kill them outright but to torture them while they continued to live and breathe. I'd never thought of it that way before."

Winter waited. She hoped the recorder on her phone hidden in her pocket was picking all of this up clearly.

Cybil stared at the blade in her hand before looking back into Winter's eyes. "Erik set up the Paymo account that could be tracked back to Dr. Poole. Erik came up with the plan to send Dr. Poole away for the rest of her miserable life. Erik, excuse me...*the Watcher* came up with the verbiage for the blackmail notes. That wacko is smarter than he looks. And all I had to do was follow his instructions to get revenge on Dr. Poole. And I did. I got it." Her expression was triumphant. "She's ruined."

"Cybil." Noah's voice was like warm milk. He was clearly trying to bring the woman back to reality. "You need to put down the knife."

Cybil seemed deaf to his instructions, a look of delight dancing over her face. "Erik is fearless. He gave me the spark I needed to finally do something, instead of just sitting in the dark and seething. That evil jackass actually set me free."

"Do you know Carl Gardner?" Noah asked, snapping his fingers to gain her attention. "Was he working with you?"

Her gaze snapped to him. "Sounds familiar. He was the hacker guy, right? Erik said he got cold feet and dropped out of the plan."

"He's dead."

A flash of fear crossed Cybil's features before her eyes narrowed into slits. "Not surprising. Erik's dangerous. The whole thing with killing the patients and torturing you with the flyers, I just went along with it. I wasn't gonna cross him."

"Seems like you were the one being manipulated." Winter shrugged. It needed to be said.

"No." Cybil stepped closer to them both, her shoulders swaying as the knife dangled in her grip. "I went along with it because I needed someone to push me. But I don't need him anymore."

Noah lifted his gun, pointed it square at her chest. "Stop and drop the weapon."

Cybil stilled, shooting him a glance before refocusing on Winter. "I don't know what you did to piss him off, but I wouldn't want to be in your shoes. He has a lot planned for you. He's been working on it for years. And I hope you're ready, because that guy has lost all touch with reality."

That was rich, coming from her.

"Do you—"

Without warning, Cybil threw the knife like a spear at Noah's face.

Like the athlete he once was, he instinctively ducked, his arm going around Winter's waist, taking her to the floor. Winter rolled and sprang from his grip to get the knife, which had clattered to the floor. In the commotion, Cybil snatched a lamp off a table, hurling it at Noah.

The ceramic base slammed into his face as Cybil shot through the open door.

He was bleeding. A slash across his cheek.

"You okay?" Winter crawled over, knife in one hand, grabbing his with the other.

"I'm fine." He touched the superficial wound as he pulled Winter to her feet.

Dropping his hand and the knife, Winter turned and raced out the door. She spotted a flash of Cybil as she turned a corner at the end of the hall, her hair fluttering behind her.

With Noah quick at her heels, Winter put on a burst of speed.

38

I burst through the exit door and pounded down the metal stairs. Fluorescent lights flickered overhead, and my boots echoed. They were right behind me. I knew they were. Or at least Winter was. It looked like my wild Hail Mary with the lamp had actually hit the man. I'd drawn blood, though I didn't know if it hit his cheek or his eye or his neck.

I really hope it nicked an artery and he was on his way out. Or maybe it blinded him on one eye. I liked Winter, but I couldn't have that crime-fighting duo on my ass forever.

When I reached the second floor, I pushed through and ran down the hall. They'd expect me to just run all the way down to street level, so I slipped into the laundry room instead. It had its own small stairwell and exit out to the back of the building. If I went through there, I could duck down the alley and make my way west to downtown.

I smacked through another door and heard a loud grunt on the other side. An old woman with a laundry basket fell back and started swearing at me. I ignored her. My lungs had never hurt so much. I'd never run so fast.

Passing under the glowing red exit sign, I loped down the

concrete steps out into the back of the building. My feet splashed in a rainbowed splatter of oil as I leaped over a short chain-link fence and darted down the alley.

A dark car pulled into the narrow space in front of me, and the door swung open. I skittered to a stop, shuffling back and forth. A man stepped out in heavy black boots and threw back the hood of his sweatshirt. I recognized those dumb tall boots, the long dark beard, and those deep-set eyes, so like the shadows of a skull.

"Erik?" I gasped and ran toward him. "What are you doing here?"

I asked the question, but my brain knew the answer. Erik was always following Winter, always two steps behind her every move. Shit, when she surprised me at Dr. Poole's office that morning, I'd seen his car parked just down the street. I imagined he'd been watching the entire interaction with Winter and her tall hunk of a partner from the cameras he'd planted in my apartment. What a nut bag.

"Thanks for coming. We have to get the hell out of here." I tried to push past him toward the car, but he hardened his shoulder and shoved me back.

"Where the hell do you think you're going?" He looked me up and down, that ugly bottom lip curling even deeper into his mouth.

I waved my hand behind me. "You know they're up there! You've been watching me like a fucking lab rat. Let's go!"

"Who's up there? Up where?"

"Are you on drugs? You—"

Erik snatched me by the wrist and whirled me around. I stumbled, my body twisting with fear and prickling with adrenaline.

"What the hell are you doing? Let go of me!" I struggled to get out of his grasp, but he was so much stronger. He held me tight, my back pressed firmly against his chest. There was a glint of gunmetal before he raised a pistol and pressed the cold barrel against my temple.

"You wanted out." His voice was a combination of chuckle and snarl. "Isn't that right, Cybil?"

Tears burned my eyes, and my nose warmed. "Erik, please. No."

He leaned in, his breath hot on my neck as he whispered into my ear. "You told them my name."

My bladder loosened. Oh, shit. I'd told them…everything. "Please don't—"

The blast of the gunshot vibrated through my entire body, and for a moment, I wondered what he'd shot.

I tried to look, but I couldn't see anymore. I couldn't feel anything either. Not the wet oil on my feet. Not my heart pounding out of control in my chest. Not the tightness of his horrible hand on my shoulder. Nothing until a burning pain slowly coated my face and my neck.

Blood. My own white-hot blood washing over me. Drowning me.

But if Erik had shot me in the head, why was I still alive?

All at once, he released me. I fought to stay upright, but my body refused to take direction from my brain. I didn't even have the strength to stumble. I just collapsed forward, smashing into the pavement.

He leaned over me, a presence as cold and dark and unfeeling as a boulder crushing my bones into powder. He touched my hand. I tried to pull back, but all I could manage was a twitch. He put something cold in my palm and wrapped my fingers around it.

The gun. He'd given me the gun. I tried to raise it, to fire at him. To finish him off before I was finished.

But I couldn't move.

The blood was so hot, but I'd frozen solid.

Erik's footfalls on the asphalt were followed by a car door

slamming shut. A whoosh of the car driving away. No squeal of tires, nothing.

The purr of the engine faded as all feeling left my skin. But there wasn't any pain. None except the knowledge that I was dying.

After I was dead, Dr. Ava Poole would be released from prison. She'd get her practice back. She'd get a new receptionist. She'd keep on living for many, many years. And she'd never be punished for what she'd done.

I should've just killed her while I had the chance.

Winter's voice reached inside me. They were yelling. Getting closer. I wanted to scream. Tell them to hurry.

But numbness washed over me, and my thoughts went flat. The noises around me gave way to silence as I drifted into the warm, wet darkness of forever.

39

Winter sat in her office. She had a pile of paperwork in front of her that she should've been filling out, but ever since getting off the phone with Detective Harlan Lessner, all she'd been able to do was sit quietly and gaze out the window at the people passing by.

Three days had passed since she'd found Cybil lying in the alleyway with a bullet in her brain and a small-caliber gun in her hand. And for the past three days, the events that had led up to that moment had been playing like a song stuck on repeat in her head, occasionally interrupted by the image of the pretty, petite woman standing in front of her like a ghost from a Victorian novel.

Last night in her dreams, Cybil came to her covered in blood, reaching out a snow-white hand.

"You know what, Winter?" Her voice echoed like the cacophony of an unpracticed choir. *"I kind of like you. And I fucking hate him, so I'm going to tell you the truth..."*

Winter blinked and looked down at her lunch of rice and sautéed vegetables. It was stone cold. She'd heated it up twice now and had yet to take a single bite. She was having a hard time eating lately. Or sleeping. Or working. Or thinking straight.

"His name is Erik Saulson. And he hates you. He never said why."

Erik Saulson. She didn't recognize the name. And the name alone was common enough to be next to useless. But that didn't mean she'd ever give up looking.

Detective Lessner had concluded, and apparently the M.E. agreed, that Cybil Kerie had committed suicide. Gun residue was found on her hands, and the angle of the shot was consistent.

"The pressure was already getting to her," Detective Lessner said. "She'd planned on staging Perry Bick's death to look like a second suicide attempt, just like the others. But she was cracking, so she just flat-out killed him."

Winter argued the point. "But she was wielding a knife in the apartment when Noah and I confronted her. You don't bring a knife to a gunfight…especially if you already have a gun on you."

"Kerie got sloppy. Maybe the gun was in her car, which was parked in the lot behind the alley where she was found." Detective Lessner shrugged. "I dunno. Look, I can't get inside the mind of a serial killer any more than you can."

It was hard to counter that statement.

"We found the murder weapon in her apartment. A pen knife. She'd washed it, but her fingerprints were on it, as well as a tiny drop of dried blood in the serration. It's being tested now."

Winter didn't doubt it would come back as a match for Perry Bick's DNA.

"We also found the tube of red lipstick we believe she used to write the message on Bick's mirror."

"That likely belonged to Dr. Poole. I saw her use it when I first met her."

After that, Winter told Detective Lessner everything she knew about Erik Saulson.

How Cybil had met him in a chat room for *people who hate*. How Erik got her out of her shell and talked her into taking action. How Cybil wanted to take Dr. Poole down, but Saulson was the one with the plan and the grudge against Winter. He was the one following her. He was the one who sent her the letter composed of cutouts from a newspaper. And how Saulson was the one pulling the strings on Carl Gardner all along. Cybil Kerie did not know why, though.

Detective Lessner listened patiently and, with a copy of the recording she'd made of the conversation sent to his email, promised to look into it.

And that was that.

A knock at her door caused Winter to flinch. She had zoned out, staring at her rice, and hadn't seen anyone approach. For a moment, she assumed it had to be Noah. He'd gone out to buy some more security equipment for their home and office—motion sensor lights, tactical trip wires, heavier dead bolts for both doors, carbon steel expandable mesh for the windows. But he'd only just left. He shouldn't have been back so soon.

Winter rose from her desk, blinking to clear her foggy brain.

Dr. Ava Poole stood outside her door, hands folded over a small brown parcel. Her long white hair was loose, her big eyes wreathed in gray shadows. And her lips were pale, no cherry-red lipstick on them today—she'd probably never wear that color again. According to Detective Lessner, she'd only been released from custody last night.

Stepping to the door, Winter turned the lock and pulled it open. "Hello."

Dr. Poole smiled sadly. "Might I come in?"

"Of course." She took a step back to let the lissome doctor

slip inside before closing and locking the door behind her. "What can I do for you, Dr. Poole?"

She pressed her lips together and held out the package.

"What's this?" Winter eyed it but didn't reach out a hand.

"Chocolates."

Tentatively, she took the package. Sure enough, on the top of the small box was a golden sticker that read *Goossens Finest Belgian Truffles*.

"Thank you?" She hadn't meant to make it sound like a question.

"I wanted to tell you how much I appreciate what you did." Dr. Poole clasped her hands tightly in front of her. "If it weren't for you, I'd still be locked up in that terrible place. The cops wouldn't listen to a word I said. They were certain I'd done all those horrible things. But you kept investigating until you uncovered the truth. I owe you my life."

Winter's hands tightened around the package, pulling it toward her chest. "Just doing my job."

"I think we both know it was more than that." Dr. Poole flashed her a genuine smile. "I wish I'd done more to help you. I should've done more."

She couldn't argue with that, so she just sighed and set the chocolates down on Ariel's desk. Noah's desk.

Whoever-the-hell's desk it was.

"So the blackmail letter Cybil sent you. I imagine it was about the affair you had with her father?"

Dr. Poole's controlled features darkened. She nodded very slightly. "I was still growing my practice then, but I also wanted marriage, and I thought I wanted children. Not that that's any kind of excuse. I always knew better. A man I'd been engaged to had just ripped my heart out. Cheated on me, ironically. And I was looking for someone to fill that void."

"I understand." Not really, but Winter wasn't going to pass judgment.

The doctor blinked, gathering sparkles of unshed tears on her black eyelashes. "I'll never forgive myself for what I did and how it affected Cybil. I didn't even know about her mother or her father's untimely demise."

Winter indicated a chair. "Would you like to sit?"

She shook her head. "I broke up with him before her mother took her own life and Cybil ended up with her dad. I chose my business, broke up with the man, and didn't look back. I wish I could have…" Her voice crackled. "I mean, I wish Cybil had just told me. Or just targeted me. Why did she have to…" It was clear Dr. Poole couldn't go on without falling apart, so she stopped talking.

Winter had the urge to hug her, not unlike she'd had the urge to hug Cybil when that disturbed young woman had related her sad story. There'd been no winners in that situation.

"I spoke with Leigh," Dr. Poole continued. "We were able to work through our problems when we figured out it was Cybil who'd put it in her mind that I was somehow abusing her during hypnosis. I think Cybil had a different endgame with Leigh Folke than with the others. Trying to get her to despise me and sue me and make my life a living hell. It was working, no doubt about that."

"How did Cybil do it?" Winter cocked her head. "Hypnotize your patients, I mean. I don't understand how she got the opportunity."

"Cybil knew I specialized in hypnosis. So when she was young, she started studying it. I think she'd been planning my undoing for a very long time." Dr. Poole flinched at her own words before composing herself. "She had an undergraduate degree that she supplemented with self-study. She became adept at the science of mesmerism."

"I still don't understand."

"She must've been watching me, because as soon as my former receptionist left, Cybil was there, running into me the very next day. I might be an educated woman, but don't underestimate the power of guilt. I was overtaken by actions from my past that I had buried. And I thought if I just hired Cybil, it would make up for her parents' divorce." Dr. Poole caught her breath. "For how I'd wronged her."

"Are you sure you don't need to sit down?"

She shook her head. "I trusted her. I was blinded by shame. And she's a bright girl. I gave her access to all my files, including the recordings I make of my sessions. She was able to listen to the power words I used with various clients, the techniques I used, and their deepest subconscious thoughts."

"What else?"

Dr. Poole pressed her hand to her face. "I even let her sit in. The patients trusted her easily. After she figured out which patients would be most susceptible to her manipulation, she went about grooming them."

Winter rubbed her eyes with her thumb and forefinger. "Do you always record your sessions?"

"I do it mostly so the patients themselves can listen to what they said while they're hypnotized. It can help them conceptualize the experience in a different way. Bringing the subconscious mind into conscious understanding can be a very powerful therapeutic tool. It also builds trust if I maintain that kind of transparency." Sighing, Dr. Poole shifted her weight between her feet. "Cybil had access to my accounts, my passwords, my email addresses, my patients, and me."

"But where and when did she hypnotize them?"

"I was looking into my records last night after I was released." Dr. Poole pressed her pale lips into a thin line. "I discovered that Cybil had been writing my schedule and the patient schedules separately. I mean, she'd give me one time for a patient's appointment and give the patient a wholly different time, often an hour or more earlier."

"Why?"

Dr. Poole's artfully drawn brows pulled together. "You see, that gave her time alone with them in the waiting room, when she could endear herself further, get into their heads, hypnotize them, and implant whatever she wanted into their subconscious. She was so good at it, she even had me believing some of the lies they told me. Such a waste of talent."

Winter narrowed her eyes at that comment. It seemed like Dr. Poole related to Cybil Kerie on some level. Clearly, she felt responsible for the trauma in Cybil's childhood and the way she'd turned out as an adult. Maybe if things had been different, Cybil could've been a world-class psychologist in her own right.

But there was no point in dwelling on that. Wondering what might've been was a road that led only to misery and madness.

"Convenient that you had a job opening."

"Yeah, a stroke of bad luck there, I guess."

"Have you ever heard the name Erik Saulson?" Winter watched Dr. Poole's features closely for any hint of recognition. "Or did you ever see Cybil talking to a tallish white man with dark hair and a bushy beard?"

She couldn't be one-hundred-percent certain the "Erik" Noah had met in the park who fit that description was Cybil's Erik, the man who'd made it his purpose in life to destroy Winter and everything she loved. All she had to go on was a very common name—an internet search turned up nothing—and Noah saying he'd gotten a funny feeling from the whole encounter.

Lacking any other evidence, Noah's feelings were good enough for her.

The doctor shook her head. "I never saw Cybil associating with anyone. Then again, it's not as if I kept a close eye on her. I trusted her."

"Thank you for coming by." Winter tapped the box of chocolates. "And thank you for this."

Dr. Poole gave another weak smile. "Thank you for clearing my name. If I can help you with anything else, please don't hesitate to contact me. I promise I'll be more forthcoming in the future."

"I will." They shook hands, and Winter unlocked the door to let Dr. Poole out.

Alone in the office again, she sat down at the reception desk. She didn't have an appetite for regular food, but who could say no to the finest Belgian truffles? Certainly not Winter Black.

She tore open the package to find a lacquered wooden box inside and a white envelope sitting on top. Winter ripped the seal with her fingertip and inside found a single piece of paper—a check for ten thousand dollars from the office of Dr. Ava Poole. In the memo line was written, *For detective services rendered.*

"What do you know?" Winter smiled and rubbed her thumb over the flourished signature. "Guess I was getting paid after all."

40

With a Belgian truffle melting like ambrosia in her cheek, Winter made her way out toward her SUV. She'd finally decided to give in to the fact that she simply couldn't focus. Every little noise made her twitch, ramping up a dull headache that had begun at the back of her neck and was spreading to her temples. She needed a break, maybe a bubble bath. She'd earned it.

She sent Noah a text, telling him to meet her at home when he was done shopping, and walked the block and a half to where she'd parked her vehicle. As expected, construction had spread into her neighborhood, making it impossible to find a space in front of her office. And it seemed the street was going to be ripped up for a very long time. She might as well get used to getting a few extra steps a day.

As she turned the corner and her dust-covered Honda came into view, Winter noticed a white paper stuffed under a wiper blade on her windshield. She froze in place, as if she'd just stepped in deep mud.

Probably just a parking ticket. She glanced over her shoulder and down the sidewalk at each of the other cars.

Several people were milling about, and the loud, pounding shrill of construction equipment jangled the environment. Dust particles floated around in the air. An ordinary scene from an ordinary day.

Winter forced her feet into action, jogging to the SUV because she couldn't bear to walk. When she realized the paper was actually a large envelope and not a flimsy sheet of transparent carbon paper, her parking ticket theory went out the window.

After checking her cargo space, her back seat, and her undercarriage, Winter ducked into the passenger's seat and grabbed two latex gloves from the glove compartment. She pulled them over her hands, snatched up the envelope, got into the driver's seat, and shut the door.

The weight of the envelope told her there was more than a piece of paper inside. It wasn't sealed—the flap was simply tucked in. No words on it, no name. With a deep breath, she pushed it open and pulled out a small stack of four-by-six glossy color pictures.

Her stomach dropped as she righted them and glared at the image on the first one. She recognized herself sitting at a restaurant dining table, a glass of wine in her hand, a bright smile on her face. Noah was at her side, looking dapper with a fork in his grasp. There was a leaf in the foreground, like whoever had taken the photo had been hiding behind foliage.

It took her a moment to put two and two together. Her heart beat fast, and she found herself glancing here and there and in all her mirrors, waiting for the attack to come. She flicked to the next picture where she and Noah were sitting in a theater. The picture was taken from behind while the house lights were up.

They were photos from the night she and Noah had gone out to celebrate his sabbatical. She flicked through two more photos of both of them—leaving the bar arm in arm and then

Winter waiting on the front porch as Noah used his keys to unlock the door.

In every single picture, somebody had taken a red sharpie and drawn a rudimentary bullseye over her. On her face, her back, her chest.

Panic prickled in her fingertips as she snatched the .38 Special revolver from her ankle holster. The maniac could be watching her at that very moment. He probably was—either physically following her or staring at her through one of his seemingly endless cameras. There was no denying he knew what he was doing. Surveilling two FBI agents without them noticing wasn't exactly an easy trick.

Her phone beeped with a notification, and Winter nearly jumped out of her skin. She hoped it would be Noah, telling her he was on his way home.

Private number.

Winter took a deep breath. Clenching the gun in her right hand—but holding it out of sight so as not to alarm any passersby—she swiped the screen open with her left index finger.

A voice memo was waiting. It felt like déjà vu. A little while back, when Carl Gardner was still active—before Noah and the FBI raided his office, and he was consequently killed in the scuffle—Winter had been receiving threatening text messages from private numbers nearly every day. When she opened them, they had a nasty tendency to disappear off her phone, as if they'd never been there in the first place.

With this in mind, Winter first took a screenshot to save the unknown number and then downloaded the file to her internal memory before uploading it to two places in the cloud. Only when she felt like she'd properly protected the number did she click the message open.

For a moment, there was nothing but static, until a strange and wet-sounding male voice came on the line.

"Well played, Winter. You cheesed your way right through Cybil's silly little game like I knew you would. She was just bullet fodder anyway. That's right, I killed her. And I killed Opal. And I'll kill you, too, when I'm good and ready. Don't try to rush it, bitch, and don't you dare try to stop me. You've got a lot of leveling up to do first."

Noah had said the Erik he met in the park was peculiar. He'd nailed that.

"Your baby brother left some pretty big shoes to fill. I've read everything there is to know about him, and challenge accepted. But you're not like Justin. You still seem to think it's worth fighting on the losing side. He tried to show you, but you've been lagging behind, grinding away, building up your pointless little life. But I'm going to show you the good side of being bad. I promise."

The voice message ended, and just like she'd predicted, both it and the number that had sent it auto-deleted from her phone, leaving nothing behind but a generic error code.

Winter's fingers shook as she checked the folder on the cloud where she'd saved the message. It was still there.

Exhaling slowly, Winter dropped the phone in her lap and leaned over the steering wheel. She wasn't someone who often felt sorry for herself, but sometimes it was almost impossible not to, especially when she was forced to think about Justin. Would she ever be able to live her life free from the constant threat of the off-brand deranged serial killers her brother's actions spawned?

That was beginning to feel like a pipe dream.

Winter picked up the photos again and flicked through another picture of her buying a mocha latte at her favorite local joint, again with that horrible red bullseye over her face.

Then she flipped to the last picture, and froze.

It was Noah, sitting on a bench, green grass all around,

trees in the background. The park. His eyes and mouth had been scratched out.

Winter dropped the stack of photos onto the passenger seat and snatched up her phone. Noah hadn't texted back. She called him and waited, her hand pounding impatiently on the steering wheel as it rang and rang.

No answer.

He'd said he was going to run home to check the measurements on their doors and windows before going to the hardware store to buy his massive haul of security equipment. He had to be in one place or the other.

She called again, every ring sending her pulse skittering faster.

No answer.

Firing up the engine, Winter veered onto the road. She called him again and again. She just needed to hear his voice. Needed to know he was okay.

No answer.

The End
To be continued...

Thank you for reading.
All of the Winter Black Series books can be found on Amazon.

ACKNOWLEDGMENTS

The past few years have been a whirlwind of change, both personally and professionally, and I find myself at a loss for the right words to express my profound gratitude to those who have supported me on this remarkable journey. Yet, I am compelled to try.

To my sons, whose unwavering support has been my bedrock, granting me the time and energy to transform my darkest thoughts into words on paper. Your steadfast belief in me has never faltered, and watching each of you grow, welcoming the wonderful daughters you've brought into our family, has been a source of immense pride and joy.

Embarking on the dual role of both author and publisher has been an exhilarating, albeit challenging, adventure. Transitioning from the solitude of writing to the dynamic world of publishing has opened new horizons for me, and I'm deeply grateful for the opportunity to share my work directly with you, the readers.

I extend my heartfelt thanks to the entire team at Mary Stone Publishing, the same dedicated group who first recognized my potential as an indie author years ago. Your collective efforts, from the editors whose skillful hands have polished my words to the designers, marketers, and support staff who breathe life into these books, have been instrumental in resonating deeply with our readers. Each of you plays a crucial role in this journey, not only nurturing my growth but also ensuring that every story reaches its full potential. Your dedication, creativity, and finesse have been nothing short of invaluable.

However, my deepest gratitude is reserved for you, my beloved readers. You ventured off the beaten path of traditional publishing to embrace my work, investing your most precious asset—your time. It is my sincerest hope that this book has enriched that time, leaving you with memories that linger long after the last page is turned.

With all my love and heartfelt appreciation,

Mary

ABOUT THE AUTHOR

Nestled in the serene Blue Ridge Mountains of East Tennessee, Mary Stone crafts her stories surrounded by the natural beauty that inspires her. What was once a home filled with the lively energy of her sons has now become a peaceful writer's retreat, shared with cherished pets and the vivid characters of her imagination.

As her sons grew and welcomed wonderful daughters-in-law into the family, Mary's life entered a quieter phase, rich with opportunities for deep creative focus. In this tranquil environment, she weaves tales of courage, resilience, and intrigue, each story a testament to her evolving journey as a writer.

From childhood fears of shadowy figures under the bed to a profound understanding of humanity's real-life villains, Mary's style has been shaped by the realization that the most complex antagonists often hide in plain sight. Her writing is characterized by strong, multifaceted heroines who defy traditional roles, standing as equals among their peers in a world of suspense and danger.

Mary's career has blossomed from being a solitary author to establishing her own publishing house—a significant milestone that marks her growth in the literary world. This expansion is not just a personal achievement but a reflection of her commitment to bring thrilling and thought-provoking stories to a wider audience. As an author and publisher, Mary continues to challenge the conventions of the thriller genre, inviting readers into gripping tales filled with serial killers, astute FBI agents, and intrepid heroines who confront peril with unflinching bravery.

Each new story from Mary's pen—or her publishing house—is a pledge to captivate, thrill, and inspire, continuing the legacy of the imaginative little girl who once found wonder and mystery in the shadows.

Discover more about Mary Stone on her website.
www.authormarystone.com

- facebook.com/authormarystone
- x.com/MaryStoneAuthor
- goodreads.com/AuthorMaryStone
- bookbub.com/authors/mary-stone
- pinterest.com/MaryStoneAuthor
- instagram.com/marystoneauthor

Printed in Great Britain
by Amazon